JIMMY WATCHED AS LUKE ROLLED their mother over. The front of her pretty blue dress was coated in mud and her own blood.

She had been shot in the back.

"Mother?" Luke said, his voice shaking.

"Benson," she whispered, opening her eyes weakly. "Hide from him."

"He's not here," Luke said. "We chased him and his men off."

She nodded, seemingly satisfied with that. She coughed, blood coming out of the corner of her mouth. She looked up at Jimmy and smiled, then back at Luke. "Take care of each other."

Jimmy watched as she closed her eyes and her body relaxed.

All the life seemed to leave her.

"Mother!" Luke shouted, his voice swallowed by the vast wilderness around them.

Their mother was dead.

They were alone.

THE LIFE AND TIMES OF
BUFFALO JIMMY

HEADED WEST

DEAN WESLEY SMITH

wmgPUBLISHING

The Life and Times of Buffalo Jimmy Headed West

Published 2015 by WMG Publishing
www.wmgpublishing.com
Book and cover design copyright © 2015 by WMG Publishing
Cover design by Allyson Longueira/WMG Publishing
Cover art copyright © Philcold/Dreamstime
Interior art copyright © Boconofist/Dreamstime

First published in *Smith's Monthly* (WMG Publishing) as a serialized novel
beginning in October 2013

THE LIFE
AND TIMES OF
BUFFALO
JIMMY

HEADED WEST

★ PART ONE ★
A GREAT LOSS

THE FIRST SHOT RIPPED INTO nineteen-year-old Jimmy Gray's saddle with a sickening thud, barely missing his right leg.

The sound of the shot echoed over the rolling Missouri hills and died into the clear, sunny afternoon air. His horse reared and threatened to bolt even though the shot had not gone through the thick leather, but Jimmy fought it back into control, spinning around completely on ridgeline covered by prairie grass.

A second shot knocked Jimmy's brother, Luke, off his horse.

Jimmy dove for the ground and cover as a third shot narrowly missed him, the sound of the bullet whistling past his ear.

He lay on the ground, face pressed into the soft dirt and grass, trying to breathe. His heart was racing. He had never been so scared in all his life.

He had never been shot at before. He read about such things in dime novels and in the newspapers, but reading about it and having it happen to you were two very different things.

Jimmy and his family were two days ride from Independence, Missouri. He and his brother had just come over the ridge two hundred paces above their family's wagon. Five men had been down there near the back of the wagon, off their horses, from what Jimmy could tell in the quick glimpse before the shooting had started

He hadn't seen his parents.

That scared him even more than being shot at. He just hoped they weren't hurt.

And was Luke hurt? He had to find out.

He had to move.

Jimmy couldn't believe this was even happening. All Jimmy had wanted to see was buffalo. Since his teacher a year ago back in Boston, in his last year of high school, had told him stories of the great buffalo hunts, Jimmy had been focused on little else. The big beasts had become an obsession, his mother had said. His father had only laughed and promised that Jimmy would see his share of buffalo by the time they reached the Wyoming Territory.

His older brother, Luke, had told him as they rode out of camp that the buffalo were no longer in Missouri in 1866, at least not this part of it. They had all been killed or driven hundreds of miles away from the wagon trail, but Jimmy didn't care. He still had his mind set on seeing a buffalo and proving Luke wrong. For all he knew, there could be an entire herd just over the next ridge.

After riding fast away from the well-worn wagon road for a half-mile or so, they had scared up rabbits. Luke, who was twenty, had the family rifle. He had become a great shot and had managed to get three rabbits with only five shots. Jimmy was an expert shot as well. Once Luke even had admitted he was better than Luke, a real natural with a gun.

Jimmy had helped Luke skin the rabbits and then they had headed back. Luke had been sick since leaving Kansas City and was riding slowly. Jimmy could tell that both of his parents were worried about Luke making the long trip across the country, but Jimmy' father had a job offer at a bank in San Francisco, and had bought a gold mining claim in the mountains near Sacramento, so the family was set on making the trip and starting a new life in the west.

It had been such a perfect, spring day.

Until the shots.

What had happened?

Jimmy scrambled on all fours through the grass, his head low, until he finally managed to reach his brother.

Luke was pushing himself up slightly on his elbows and blood was streaming from his leg. "Get the rifle off my saddle," he said through gritted teeth. "Quick!"

Jimmy glanced around.

Luke's horse had only gone about twenty paces back from the top of the ridge and then stopped. Keeping his head down, Luke ran for the horse, grabbed the rifle from the saddle and brought it back.

There were no more shots at him coming from their wagon, but off his horse, Jimmy couldn't see the trail over the edge of the rise, which meant the men doing the shooting couldn't see him.

Luke had torn off the bottom of his shirt and wrapped it around his leg, but it didn't look to Jimmy as if the bleeding had slowed much.

Luke grabbed the rifle from Jimmy, cocked it to make sure it was loaded, then staying low, hopped the few steps to the top of the ridge, dragging his bad leg behind him.

Jimmy stayed beside him, and at the top of the ridge they both lay down in the grass and crawled the last few feet so they could see the trail below.

Jimmy was shocked at what faced them. He wanted to jump and run, but somehow stayed beside Luke.

Two men on horseback were riding up the hill toward them, guns drawn. Three other men were pulling things from the wagon and scattering them on the ground. Jimmy had no idea where his parents were.

He and Luke were going to die, Jimmy was sure of that.

This was just like all the bad stories he had heard about the western frontier coming true right now.

His stomach was so twisted up, he could hardly breathe.

"Keep your head down," Luke whispered.

Then, taking a deep breath, Luke pulled down on the men like he was shooting rabbits. The shot exploded in Jimmy's ear, since he was so close to Luke.

The lead man went over backwards off his horse like a trick rider Jimmy had seen at the Circus last year in Boston.

The other man's horse reared up, and by the time he could get turned around, Luke fired again.

He must have missed. The second man took off back down the hill toward the wagon. The man that Luke had shot pushed himself to his feet, holding his stomach, and then half-ran, half-staggered back down the hill.

The three men below had their guns out and were firing up at Luke and Jimmy.

"Keep your head down," Luke ordered again. Then he fired back at the men around the wagon. Jimmy watched one of Luke's shots splinter wood off the wagon bed right beside one man.

Luke shot again and another of the men danced as the bullet kicked up dirt and mud right at his feet.

Luke didn't hit any of the men, but his next shot, and the one after, sent them scrambling for their horses.

Jimmy recognized one of the men.

Jake Benson, the man his father had hired to guide them from Kansas City to Independence.

The three men quickly mounted up and joined the fourth. He had picked up the wounded man and was riding at full speed down the trail toward Independence. The horse of the man Luke had shot grazed on the side of the hill. Clearly, they didn't have the stomach for a fight in the open for a horse with Luke having the rifle and the upper ground and all they had were pistols.

Jimmy watched them go, their dust kicking up small clouds behind them.

It seemed to take an eternity for them to vanish over the distant rise.

When would they be back? The question made Jimmy shudder.

The wagon still sat where Jimmy and Luke had left it when they had left to go hunting. It was sitting just off to one side of the muddy tracks of the wagon road, with their two secondary horses grazing while still in harness. But the lunch fire was smoldering instead of burning, and a lot of their personal things had been tossed out into the dirt and dried mud.

After all the shooting, the silence of the wide-open prairie was broken only by the light breeze through the grass.

Tomb-like silent.

Luke sat up, checked his wound, then pushed himself to his feet.

"Get our horses," he said to Jimmy.

Jimmy turned and ran for their two horses, the fear of what might have happened to his parents twisting at his stomach like a bad belly-ache. He grabbed Luke's horse, then mounted up on his own, the hole where the bullet had embedded in the leather of his saddle a clear reminder of just how close he had come to getting shot.

By the time he got back to his brother, Luke's face looked white, and it was clear that he was in a lot of pain.

"Let's find Mother and Father," Luke said, reaching for his horse's reins.

Jimmy made sure Luke could get back on his horse, then started down the hill ahead of his older brother, working to keep his hands from shaking and his stomach under control while trying to look in a thousand directions at the same time for Benson and his men. They would be back. He had no doubt.

The wind whistled lightly in his ears under his hat, the warm afternoon sun glared in his eyes. He forced himself to take shallow breaths as the ride seemed to stretch into an eternity.

It wasn't until he had moved almost halfway down the hill that he saw what he had feared the most. His mother and father were lying in the mud near the rear wheels of the wagon. Neither seemed to be moving.

Jimmy dismounted ten running steps from the wagon before the horse had even stopped.

An instant later he was on his knees beside his father.

He was dead.

His blood had made a muddy pool, his eyes were staring up, unseeing at the blue sky and light white clouds. He had been shot at least twice.

Jimmy stared at the man who had always been there for him. His father couldn't be dead. He was too strong, too powerful a man to die.

An instant later, Luke was on the ground beside their mother.

Jimmy watched as Luke rolled her over. The front of her pretty blue dress was coated in mud and her own blood.

She had been shot in the back.

As Luke rolled her over, she blinked, then opened her eyes.

She was alive!

For a moment, it was clear she wasn't aware of where she was, but as Jimmy moved closer, she looked up at Luke.

"Mother?" Luke said, his voice shaking.

Jimmy touched her arm, trying to give her some comfort as well. He had no idea what they could do.

"Benson," she whispered. "Hide from him."

"He's not here," Luke said. "We chased him and his men off."

She nodded, seemingly satisfied with that. She coughed, blood coming out of the corner of her mouth. She looked up at Jimmy and smiled, then back at Luke. "Take care of each other."

Jimmy watched as she closed her eyes and her body relaxed.

All the life seemed to leave her.

"Mother!" Luke shouted, his voice swallowed by the vast wilderness around them.

Their mother was dead.

They were alone.

⋆ PART TWO ⋆
MOVING FORWARD

JIMMY HAD NO IDEA HOW long he had sat beside the wagon road alternating between staring at his parents' bodies and watching the trail and hills for Benson to come back.

Maybe minutes. Maybe hours.

He didn't know. But finally, the cold afternoon wind made him realize he and Luke had to move.

Luke had crawled a few feet from the bodies and just lay on his back, the rifle at his side. Jimmy couldn't tell if he had passed out, or was just staring up into the sky. The shirt tied around his leg was bright red with blood.

Jimmy found a sheet one of the men had tossed out of the wagon. He ripped out bandage-length strips, then found a bottle of his father's best whisky and, with a quick check for Benson and his men, moved over to his brother.

Luke didn't protest as Jimmy unwrapped the bloody shirt, tore open his pants a little near the wound and checked how bad it was.

The bleeding had mostly stopped and the bullet had gone all the way through. That was lucky, but Jimmy still had to get Luke to a doctor and soon.

He poured some whiskey on the wound, as he had seen his father do when Jimmy's mother had cut her hand.

Luke winced, but didn't say anything. He didn't even open his eyes. Then Jimmy wrapped the wound in the clean strips from the sheet.

"We have to get you fixed up," Jimmy said, his voice breaking the silence of the vast plain.

The wind seemed to pull his words away over the swaying grassland almost as he spoke them.

Luke didn't move.

Jimmy pushed himself to his feet and then, without looking at his parents' bodies, he climbed into the back of their wagon and pulled out two of his mother's favorite blankets, then got the two shovels his father had bought in St. Louis and went back out into the sun and breeze. He tossed one shovel onto the ground beside Luke. Then he covered his father with a blanket, then his mother.

"Luke, I'm going to start digging some graves up on the top of the rise. I should be able to see if Benson and his men are doubling back from up there. Rest as long as you need to."

Luke shook his head. "We stay together."

Luke took a deep breath and pushed himself to his feet, using the shovel to balance on one leg. The sickness he had been fighting since they left Boston had really made him weak, and now getting shot had made him much worse. Even though Jimmy was the youngest, he was going to have to be the strongest until Luke got better.

Together, with Jimmy keeping guard and carrying the rifle, they slowly moved up the hill through the grass, Luke using one shovel as a crutch.

At the top, at a place that seemed to overlook the vast plains, they started to dig through the thick sod and into the wet, damp ground.

It would be a good final resting place for their parents.

Jimmy had no idea how long they had been digging, but every few minutes he kept watch, and finally, he saw something. Three wagons were moving toward them slowly but steadily, coming from St. Louis.

"We have company," Jimmy said. "Wagons. Not Benson."

He felt a little relieved. As his father had always said, there was safety in numbers out west. Benson and his men might still attack them, but with other wagons close by, it wasn't likely.

Luke stopped and leaned on his shovel. He was breathing hard and sweating far more than he should have. Bright red blood spotted the bandages on his leg.

"They'll go around," Luke said, and went back to digging.

Jimmy watched his brother for a moment. They had not made that much headway on the two graves, and Jimmy doubted Luke was going to be able to keep going much longer. If they were going to do this right, and give their parents a proper resting place, and be safe from Benson, they were going to need help.

"I'm going to see if they'll lend a hand," Jimmy said. "You rest."

"I don't need rest," Luke said.

"I don't plan on burying you as well," Jimmy said, turning back to glare at his brother. Then with his sternest voice, he said, "Now rest and I'll go talk to these people."

Luke stared at Jimmy for a moment, then nodded and dropped to the ground. A moment later he was lying on his back, his eyes closed, the family rifle in one hand.

In all his life, Jimmy had never felt so alone.

His parents dead, his older brother injured and sick. He was in charge.

How could he be in charge of anything? He was only nineteen.

He first gathered up the killer's horse, then the two horses that he and Luke had been riding. Luckily, they hadn't gone far and were just grazing near the trail. He tied them to the wagon, constantly keeping watch for Benson and his men.

Then he started down the wagon trail, walking beside the deepest ruts toward the oncoming wagons. The three wagons were spaced a good distance apart, and all seemed to be what was called a "small wagon" with square canvas tops, similar to the one his parents had purchased.

A man about his father's age was driving the first rig, moving a team of four oxen gently forward. A woman and two younger children were walking along to one side of the wagon, and a fifth oxen and a horse were tied to the back. The other two wagons also seemed to have families, but they were far enough back that Jimmy couldn't tell for sure.

"What can I do for you, mister?" the man said, stopping his wagon with the lead oxen about twenty paces from Jimmy.

Jimmy stopped as well. He didn't want to seem threatening in any way.

The woman moved up beside her husband and stared at Jimmy, holding her two younger children behind her skirt.

"We were robbed and my parents were killed, sir." Jimmy made himself go on after that sentence. "By the man we hired to guide us to Independence. My brother and I were out hunting. My brother's also been shot and is not very strong, since he's recovering from being sick. If you might stop for a short time, we could sure use the help in burying our parents."

"Oh, my," the woman said before her husband could get out a word.

11

"Of course we'll help," he said, nodding. "We'll pull around you and stop." He turned to his wife. "Go back and tell the other wagons what we are doing."

"Thank you," Jimmy said. "Very much appreciated." He turned and walked ahead of the wagons back toward the hill. He didn't allow himself to look at the blankets behind his wagon.

"They're going to help," he said to Luke as he reached the top of the hill, picked up his shovel, and went back to digging. "And with them helping, we'll be safer for the moment."

Luke only sighed and didn't move.

★ PART THREE ★
INDEPENDENCE

IT TOOK TWO DAYS TO make the trip into Independence, following the other three wagons as part of their group. Luke had just laid in the bed of the wagon most of the trip, seemingly getting sicker and weaker by the day, even though one of the women from the wagons had nursing training from the war and had cleaned Luke's wound and got it to stop bleeding.

Jimmy had driven the team, taken care of the horses each night, and done what little cooking they needed. Luke didn't eat much, and Jimmy hadn't felt hungry either. He just felt numb.

Luckily, his father had spent a few hours teaching him how to handle the wagon and the horses, but he clearly wasn't that good, and a few simple stream crossings had almost turned disastrous. Henry Basker, the man he had first talked to in the lead wagon, had finally, on what looked like a really nasty downhill crossing, offered to take the wagon across for Jimmy and show him how to do it. Jimmy had never felt so relieved in his life.

Every mile of the trip, he kept expecting Benson and his men to come charging in and kill them all. Jimmy had told Basker and the other two men about Benson and his men, so all of the men on the wagons rode with their guns at the ready.

During the first night of camp, with Luke asleep in a tent beside the wagon, Jimmy had dug through what was left of their family's possessions. Benson had stolen the supply money his father planned to use in Independence and his mother's family jewelry. And worse yet, Benson had stolen the gold mine deed.

The entire family had all been excited about that mine when his father first told them about buying the deed. Ever since Jimmy could remember, people had talked about finding gold out west and never having to work again. Now his father had bought them a real gold mine.

The plan was for his father to work in the bank while Jimmy and Luke worked the mine. Jimmy knew he couldn't get the money or jewelry back from Benson. Those would be gone before they caught up with him. But Benson would hold onto that deed, not knowing how much it was worth, and Jimmy figured that if he found Benson, he and Luke could get the mine back.

To make the deed be worth anything, Benson would have to register his ownership of the deed in Sacramento, just as his father had been planning to do. Jimmy and Luke had to make sure they got to Sacramento before Benson, or get the deed back along the way somewhere.

If Benson didn't come and kill them first, that is.

In his search of the wagon that first night, Jimmy was very relieved to find that Benson hadn't found the false bottom of a family chest his mother had insisted they bring along. In that false bottom, his father had put the money he planned on using to buy them a new home in San Francisco.

Jimmy had strapped a third of the money in a cloth holder to the small of his back under his shirt, then left part of the rest in the false chest bottom, and some more in a false bottom in the wagon floor.

By the time they arrived outside of Independence and stopped the wagon with what looked to be thousands of other wagons, it was around noon of the third day since the shooting.

Jimmy left their wagon camped on a wide plain a mile to the north of Independence next to the Basker wagon, then took Luke into town to find a doctor.

Luke was so sick, he could barely ride, and Jimmy had to stop three times along the well-traveled road to let Luke rest.

Independence was far larger than Jimmy had expected, seeming to spread out over two small hills and fill a broad valley. The wide main streets were so crowded, it was hard to even walk a horse up the middle of them. The streets were muddy and smelled of horse manure. The sidewalks were wood and slippery from spring rains and mud tracked up from the street.

The excitement of being in a new place, a vibrant, alive place like Independence, was shocking. It felt like a large carnival, with lots of noise, loud talking, and construction sounds. Piano music came from the open doors of dozens of saloons, and men fighting in the mud seemed to be common.

Everyone, no matter what age, seemed to have an intense purpose, and no one noticed the two brothers at all, at least that Jimmy could see.

Jimmy, on constant alert for Benson, went into town from the side, staying off the main streets, and tied the horses off on a side street near a saloon. With Luke leaning on him, he managed to walk along the wooden sidewalk and get into a doctor's office beside a general store.

In town, he felt a lot safer with all the people around him, but he still didn't want Benson to know he and Luke were here.

The doctor, a friendly, older man named Davis, stood about as tall as Jimmy's five-ten, but had a pot belly on him that made him look almost round. He wore glasses and his brown hair was thin and long, combed over to one side.

Doc Davis took one look at Luke, touched his hot forehead, and had Jimmy help him get Luke in a bed in the back of the office, beside two other sick men and a sick child.

"What happened?" Doc Davis asked Jimmy after Luke was resting.

"We were coming with our parents," Jimmy said. "Ambushed by robbers. Parents are dead." He was shocked at how that sounded. It still didn't seem right that they were gone.

"They shot Luke in the leg before we ran them off."

"I'm so sorry," Doc Davis said, putting his hand gently on Jimmy's shoulder.

"Luke and I can get by all right," Jimmy said, taking a deep breath and squaring his shoulders. He pulled a coin out of his pants pocket to pay the doctor. "Will this be enough to get Luke well?" He gave the doctor the twenty dollar gold piece.

Doc Davis looked at it, clearly surprised, then nodded and put it in his pocket. "More than enough. We'll take good care of him, I can promise you that. Do you have a place to stay?"

"I have the family wagon outside of town," Jimmy said. "I'll be staying there."

Doc Davis brushed his thinning hair to one side of his head. "If you need anything, you just come to me. Understand? And I'll let you know more tomorrow on how Luke is doing."

Jimmy nodded. "Thanks, Doctor. I'll be back tomorrow."

With that, Jimmy stepped back out onto the street of the busy western town.

Alone.

His parents dead, his brother sick, and he was alone in a strange town. He had told his friends in Boston he wanted to go west for the adventure.

He just hadn't dreamed it would be like this.

★ PART FOUR ★
LUKE'S CONDITION

THE NEXT DAY, DOC DAVIS had said that there was no improvement in Luke's health, and he didn't really know what was wrong.

And he said the same thing the next day as well. "He just needs to rest."

The two days had been filled with rain and cold winds. Jimmy had spent much of the last two days either sitting beside Luke's bed, or searching carefully around town for Benson, walking in the rain with his hat pulled down to hide his face.

Jimmy had decided that he couldn't constantly hide from Benson. It would be better if Jimmy found the killer first, and kept track of him. As long as he was in town, or with the hundreds of wagons camped out on the plain, he would be somewhat safe. But he and Luke would be a lot safer if he knew where Benson was. And if Jimmy did find him, when Luke got better, they would be able to tell the sheriff what Benson had done, and get him arrested.

During the two days, Jimmy had come to know the town of Independence pretty well, including which parts were just too dangerous for him to get near. It seemed even bigger than he had first thought. When he asked one shopkeeper how many people were here, the man had laughed and said, "At what moment? This time of the year, there has to be a hundred thousand people here and out in that sea of wagons."

How was Jimmy ever going to find one man in a city that size? It seemed impossible. And he didn't feel comfortable going into the saloons, at least not without Luke at his side. So finally, he just decided he would stand with his hat low on his forehead where he could see five or six of the biggest saloon's front doors and watch for Benson.

Jimmy knew he had to play this smart if he was going to get the justice his parents deserved and stay alive doing so. It was like a big game, with life and death as the stakes, and he was doing the best he could.

On the morning of the third day, the sun came back out enough to make the air thick and steamy. The muddy streets mixed with horse manure smelled even worse, if that was possible. Somehow, the town's people had gotten used to the smell, but Jimmy had grown up in Boston, where they paved the streets for the most part, and kept them mostly clean.

Jimmy tied up his horse at his normal spot on the side street just down from the doctor's office. With the sun out, laughter echoed everywhere along the main street. And everyone was moving at a more frantic pace, if that was possible.

Dozens of smaller trains had been leaving every day since he had arrived. A couple of the really big trains, with upwards of a hundred wagons each, were getting ready to head out, and that made him even more worried about what he was going to do next.

He had a wagon and five horses he needed to take care of. The Tasker family had been watching them while he was visiting Luke. He didn't have any help after they left.

"Hi, little brother," Luke said, smiling as Jimmy walked into the back room of the Doc's office. Luke was sitting up in bed, and seemed to have some color in his face.

Jimmy felt his mood soar even more. Suddenly, it felt like the weight of the world had lifted from his shoulders. He wanted to rush forward and just hug Luke, but somehow he stopped himself and just stood beside the bed smiling.

"He's doing better," Doc Davis said to Jimmy. "But for now, I want him to stay right here where I can watch him. He's very weak and a long way from being recovered. And with all the cholera going around, I wouldn't want him to get that in his condition."

"Thanks, Doc," Jimmy said.

Luke smiled. "Yes, thank you, for everything. Especially that young nurse you have helping you."

Doc Davis glared at Luke. "That's my daughter."

Luke's face went back to pale.

Then Doc Davis laughed a deep, rich laugh that filled the room, patted Jimmy on the shoulder again, and left, still laughing.

"He got you with that one," Jimmy said, also laughing.

"Yeah, he did," Luke said. "But she's still cute as a Sunday bonnet."

Jimmy pulled up a chair beside Luke's bed and with Luke leading the questioning, he filled in his big brother on what had happened over the last few days since they got to Independence, what the town was like, what the vast camp for wagons looked like.

The conversation felt wonderful and Jimmy was sure it was the longest the two of them had talked in a long time.

"I've been looking for Benson," Jimmy finally said, worried about what his big brother would say.

Luke looked suddenly serious and worried. "Jimmy, he and that gang of his are cold-blooded killers. I don't want you doing anything until I'm with you."

Jimmy laughed. "You don't have to worry about that. I'm just trying to find him. I won't let him see me if I do."

"Good," Luke said, sighing. "I'll be getting better soon, I promise." He settled down into the bed a little more. He was again looking tired and pale.

Jimmy pushed his chair back. "I'll let you rest and be back later this afternoon." He patted his brother's shoulder. "Glad you decided to stick around."

"Yeah, me too little brother. Me too."

★ PART FIVE ★
FINDING FRIENDS

JIMMY PULLED HIS HAT DOWN low to hide his face some, then walked out of the doc's office and into the warm, morning air, the spring back in his step. He almost felt like whistling. Pretty soon Luke would be back on his feet and helping him. And that was the best news he had had in a week. He wouldn't be alone.

He moved up the crowded sidewalk to a spot where he could see the front doors of five of the major saloons along the street, all doing a noisy business even this early in the morning. Through the windows of the closest one, he could see two card games going on, and a dozen men standing at a long bar.

He moved to the inside of the sidewalk and leaned against the rough wood wall of a lawyer's office, out of the way of all the hustle and bustle of people filling up their wagons from the dozen general stores along the street. If his mother and father had lived, more than likely he would be one of those people busy filling saddlebags and wagons with provisions.

"Which wagon you working?" a voice asked beside him.

He spun around, ready to run, his heart beating wildly in his chest. A young guy about his age was leaning against the wall. At first, Jimmy thought the blond-headed guy was older, but then his blue eyes told him he was about Jimmy's age. He had his long hair tied back and wore a buckskin jacket that clearly had seen some wear.

"I don't have a wagon here in town," Jimmy said, letting out the air he had been holding and trying to not let the guy see how scared he had been. "Just looking for someone."

The kid laughed. "I told Truitt you weren't competition. But he wanted me to ask."

"Competition for what?" Jimmy asked.

"Working the wagons," the guy said, as if Jimmy should know what that meant. "You got a family?"

"A sick brother in Doc Davis's back room," Jimmy said.

"So you're alone," the guy said, nodding. "So am I. So is my friend Truitt." The guy stuck out his hand. "I'm Zach. Zach Roy."

"Jimmy Tyler," he said, smiling at finally meeting someone besides the doc. "So, what's *working a wagon* mean?"

"Watch," Zach said and pointed at an open-topped wagon being pulled by two horses. The wagon's horses had been tied off just down the street from Hill and Stevens General Store. As Jimmy watched, a young man with chopped up brown hair and pants that were too short for him approached the wagon from along the street side, seeming to wade effortlessly in the mud.

"That's Truitt," Zach said. "Watch him closely. He's a master at working a wagon."

There was no one near the wagon. The owners must have been in the store.

Truitt had clearly timed his arrival near the stopped wagon as another wagon passed close by. As the second wagon went by, Truitt seemed to be knocked against the stopped wagon as if he had been grazed.

He caught himself against the wagon, and then almost faster than Jimmy could follow, Truitt had a bag from the back of the wagon under his arm and was heading across the street and toward a side street as if he'd always had the bag with him, walking as if nothing was different.

"Looks like a bag of beans," Zach said, smiling. "That will keep us eating for a few weeks."

"You're stealing food?" Jimmy said, turning to face Zach.

Zach just smiled and shrugged. "When you have no money, you do what you have to do."

Jimmy started to say something, then stopped. He had come very close to being in Independence without money as well. If Benson had found his father's secret stash, Jimmy would right now be thinking about how to get food and pay Doc Davis for treating Luke.

"You don't have a family?" Jimmy asked Zach as Truitt disappeared safely down the side street with his prize.

"All my family, my parents, my girl died of the cholera in St. Louis a few months back," Zach said, his voice level and cold. "I promised my dad before he died that I'd head west, carry on with the family dream. So far, this is as far as I've got."

"What about Truitt?" Jimmy asked.

Zach shrugged. "He's alone and won't talk much about it. So, since you're not working the wagons, who are you looking for?"

Jimmy decided that he could trust Zach. He didn't really know him, but he felt like he did, and for now, that was enough.

"I'm looking for the man and his gang who killed my parents. Shot my mother in the back. Two days ride back toward St. Louis."

"Oh," Zach said. "What do you plan on doing when you find him?"

"At the moment, nothing," Jimmy said. "But eventually, when my brother gets well, we'll somehow make him pay for what he's done, report him to the sheriff or something."

"Well, it's a plan," was all Zach said.

★ PART SIX ★
BUILDING A GANG

LUKE'S HEALTH SEEMED TO LEVEL over the next two days. He didn't get better, but he didn't get worse, either. They had talked a lot about different things, including what to do with the wagon and horses when the Tasker family left. So far, they hadn't come up with any solution.

Each day, while looking for Benson, Jimmy had run into Zach and Truitt. He had come to like them both, but refused to help them work a wagon. He didn't much like the idea of stealing, and at the moment he didn't need to in order to eat and take care of Luke.

It was on the afternoon of the second day, when there weren't enough wagons on the street to make it safe to work them, that a new opportunity arose. Two drunks had staggered out of a bar and gone down a narrow alley to either be sick or pass out. To Jimmy's surprise, the moment Zach and Truitt saw the two drunks, they laughed and said almost together, "Time to roll a drum."

Jimmy decided he actually didn't want to know what that meant, so he stayed in his spot watching the saloon doors while Zach and Truitt moved across the muddy street and to the alley that cut between two buildings. It was too narrow for a wagon and it looked like it held nothing but garbage and broken furniture from a nearby bar.

As Jimmy watched, Zach and Truitt approached the two drunks. Zach said something, then reached down to touch the one drunk. The next moment, the man had a gun in his hand faster than Jimmy could ever imagine being possible. And especially amazing for a man who seemed as drunk as that man looked.

Without losing his aim, the man climbed to his feet to face Zach.

The second man grabbed Truitt and held on while Zach backed against the wall, his hands in the air. Clearly, the two drunks knew what *rolling a drum* meant, and didn't much like it.

Jimmy started across the muddy street, not really sure what he was going to do to help, but Zach and Truitt had become his friends, so he had to help them somehow. His stomach twisted into a knot, but he kept walking, trying to think of anything that might set them free.

As he entered the alleyway, the smell of mold and vomit washed over him and made his stomach even tighter. He could hear one of the drunks threatening to shoot Zach. Some men were fun drunks, others got mean. Jimmy had seen them both in Boston. Clearly, this man was one of the mean ones.

The other drunk held Truitt pinned tight against the wood wall. This situation was going to get downright deadly in about ten seconds if Jimmy didn't do something.

And fast.

"Deputy Roy," Jimmy said loudly, pretending nothing was wrong as he walked toward the man with the gun. "Want me to call the sheriff? Seems you're having a little trouble with getting these two drunks out of this alley. But I will say, this will be a might embarrassing letting these two get the drop on you."

Zach, not missing a beat, laughed. "It sure is."

"You're going to be *dead* embarrassed, mister," the drunk holding Zach said, putting the gun under Zach's chin. "You was gonna rob me."

Jimmy decided right at that moment that he was really starting to hate guns, but he managed to laugh. "And why would you want to go and be hanged for killing a deputy on such a wonderful spring day?"

"This guy ain't no deputy," the drunk said. But even as he said that, he pulled his gun back and pointed it slightly upward. Clearly Jimmy had confused him.

"He sure is," another voice said from the back of the alley.

A moment later, a young guy, really short, and Jimmy figured him to be no more than eighteen years old, even though he looked younger, stepped out of the shadows and moved right up to Zach. He grabbed Zach around the middle and hugged him. "He's my dad. You wouldn't want to kill my dad, would you?"

By this point, Jimmy could tell the drunk was getting really confused. And overwhelmed. Actually, Jimmy was confused as well, but he kept playing the hand he had started.

"Deputy Roy, when did you start letting your son play in the alleys?" Jimmy asked.

"He's not supposed to be here," Zach said, following right along.

Then, while the drunk with the gun stared in amazement at Zach and the young kid holding him like he really was his daddy, another man with long black hair braided into a ponytail stepped out of the shadows and hit the second drunk with a chair leg.

The crack echoed through the narrow alley.

The drunk let go of Truitt and slumped to the ground with a loud moan.

The first drunk spun around, for the first time pointing the gun away from Zach.

The young kid, getting almost airborne, kicked the man's gun hand hard.

The gun went flying into the shadows, landing in something that sounded very wet and very sloppy.

"Ow!" the drunk shouted and held his injured hand against his chest. "Mister, I'll kill you for that."

Zach stepped forward and punched the guy once in the stomach.

When the guy doubled over, the kid with the long braided hair hit him with the chair leg.

The younger-looking kid searched one drunk's pockets while Truitt looked through the others, then all five of them headed out of the alley, across the street, and down a side street, laughing as they walked.

"Thanks," Zach said, glancing at Jimmy. "That was some quick thinking."

"I had a hard time not laughing though," said Truitt, shaking his head. "Deputy Roy. What a hoot."

"Yeah, had me laughing too," said the shorter guy who had kicked the gun.

"Thanks for the help," Zach said to the new men with them. "Who are you two?"

"I'm C.J.," the short one said as they reached a side street and turned toward the edge of town.

"Longfellow Runningwind," the other said, his voice deep and slow.

Jimmy wasn't sure, but he sounded like he had a New York accent.

29

"Call him Long," said C.J. "Just easier."

"You mind?" Zach asked and Long said no.

Jimmy looked at Long, suddenly realizing that he had just met his first Indian. Or half-Indian, more than likely.

"We better lay low for a few hours," Zach said. "We got beans and some bacon at our camp if you're interested."

Both C.J. and Long looked very interested, both nodding so fast that it was clear to Jimmy that they hadn't eaten today.

Jimmy felt almost embarrassed that he had had a good breakfast at his wagon and had money to buy provisions, at least for a little while. But he didn't say anything. He just felt good having a few friends. That hadn't happened since his last day in school in Boston. He didn't realize until now how much he missed his friends back there.

And how much safer he felt hanging around with them.

Zach and Truitt's camp was a small tent and a lean-to in a small grove of scrub brush near the edge of a small stream. More than likely, this stream would be dry in the summer, but right now, it was flowing good enough to give them some decent water. And they were upstream from the town and the mass of wagons on the other side, which made the water pretty safe to drink.

Truitt dug out some beans and a large pan and filled it with water while Zach started a fire. With the beans, Truitt put in a few scraps of bacon and a pretty good handful of salt. Then, as the beans were cooking, the five of them sat around the fire and talked.

It turned out C.J. wouldn't say anything about his family or his past, but it was clear to Jimmy that the short, blond-haired man had been to school somewhere. He wore wire-rimmed glasses and was constantly cleaning and adjusting them.

None of them wanted to talk about the war at all. Jimmy had learned early on in the trip that talking about the war was always a bad idea. Jimmy had managed to miss the war because he had been too young, and Luke had gone in, but missed most of the action.

Jimmy had also been right about Long. His mother was Sioux and his father white. Long had spent time in both worlds. He had gone to school just outside of New York and had left his mother to get away from the Indian way of life, but had also managed to stay out of the war.

As the beans were being served, C.J. admitted that it was the first meal that he and Long had had that day. They were basically living in that alley, trying to find a way to head west. They had no money, no horses, nothing to their names but clothes and an extra pair of glasses for C.J.

"Well, Jimmy," Zach said, "isn't it about time you tell us who you've been looking for?"

"Yeah?" C.J. said. "Standing out there against that wall for hours certainly draws attention to you.

Jimmy could feel his stomach twisting. "I didn't know I had been that obvious." He had been trying to stay hidden from Benson, and had actually been as obvious as a wine stain on a Sunday-go-to-church shirt.

"Maybe not to most," Truitt said, "but for those of us who watch for any small detail to help us survive, you're one dang big question mark."

Jimmy took a deep breath and managed to laugh. "All right, I'm looking for a man named Jake Benson." He quickly told them the story.

"So, where's your brother?" Long asked when Jimmy finished.

"Doc Davis's office back room."

"He getting better?" Zach asked, actually looking like he cared.

"Not much," Jimmy said. "He's going to need a lot of rest and care."

31

Suddenly, Jimmy had an idea. His father's voice rang clearly in his head. *Out west, there is safety in numbers.*

"Look," Jimmy said, "I need to go check in on my brother and talk to him about something. Are you four going to be here in an hour? If so, I've got an idea you might all like."

Zach glanced at Truitt, then at C.J. and Long.

"I am in no driving hurry to return to that alley," C.J. said.

Truitt snorted. "I couldn't agree with you more about that. Just stay here for the night."

Zach nodded. "We'll be here."

"I'll be back after I talk to my brother. And don't worry if you hear a horse approaching. That will be me."

"You have a horse?" C.J. asked, surprise on his dirty face.

"Actually," Jimmy said, smiling as he turned away. "I have five of them."

"Oh," was all he heard Zach say.

★ PART SEVEN ★
GETTING HELP

JIMMY DISMOUNTED NEAR WHERE THE others were still eating and tied up the horse on a tree limb. Luke had agreed that he should tell his friends about the wagon and have them help.

"How's your brother doing?" Zach asked.

Jimmy was surprised. It seemed that Zach actually cared.

"Very tired," Jimmy said. "We're moving him into a hotel room tomorrow so the Doc can look in on him every day and have the bed in the back free for other sick folk."

Zach and the rest nodded.

"You've got some money," C.J. said, more as a statement than a question.

"Not much," Jimmy said, telling them the truth. "Just what Benson didn't find in my parent's wagon. But enough to buy some provisions and take care of my brother until we decide what to do next."

"So, what's this idea we're going to like?" Truitt asked. "I love surprises, in case no one's told you that yet."

"I might have guessed," Jimmy said, smiling. "I've got a wagon about a mile outside of town. The people who have been watching the wagon and my stock during the day are pulling out tomorrow and I need help."

"You want us to be guards?" Zach asked, looking puzzled.

Truitt just laughed. "We take things, remember?"

Jimmy ignored him. "Actually, I was thinking you could all move out there with me. We can take turns staying with the wagon and stock and I'll pay for all the food and supplies for as long as my money lasts. No more stealing and safer than here or in that alley."

There was silence around the small campfire for a moment. From the distance, you could hear the sounds of pianos and shouting coming from the saloons, getting louder as evening got closer.

"Count me in," Zach said. "On one condition."

"What's the condition?" Jimmy asked, afraid of what it might be. He looked into the blue eyes of a guy he had really come to like over the last few days.

"If you and your brother head west, you take me with you. I promised my dad I'd head west, and this seems to be a good shot at doing just that."

"Me too," C.J. said. "I'm in with that condition."

"Oh, I so love stealing food just to survive, why would I want to join this craziness?" Truitt asked. Then he laughed. "Of course I'm in if you take me with you as well."

They all looked at Long, who just nodded. "I'll join as well. But I have one question. Are you headed for Oregon or California?"

"California," Jimmy said.

Long nodded that he liked that.

Jimmy looked around at the four friends and decided to tell them about the gold mine that Benson had taken.

34

"A gold mine?" C.J. asked, stunned when Jimmy had finished.

Truitt laughed. "I love surprises and you are sure made of them."

Jimmy smiled. "A real gold mine with a real deed that my father thought might be worth a lot of money. And my father had been a banker, so he would know."

"It seems we have an adventure ahead of us," Truitt said, clapping his hands together in sheer glee.

"You mean better than rolling a drum?" Jimmy asked.

"Far, far better," Truitt said. "Who could ask for more fun? The bunch of us heading west."

Jimmy glanced at Zach, who was smiling wider than Jimmy could imagine him ever smiling.

"Thanks," Zach said.

"Don't thank me," Jimmy said. "It's a long ways from here to Sacramento. And first we have to find Benson and somehow, without getting killed, get that mine deed back."

"If anyone can find him," C.J. said, smiling at Truitt, "we can."

⋆ PART EIGHT ⋆
THE SEARCH BEGINS

WHILE THE OTHERS HAD ROUNDED up what few possessions they had from their camps, Jimmy had ridden out and gotten two other horses, then brought all four of his new friends back to the wagon, with Truitt riding behind Zach and C.J. behind Long.

By nightfall, they had had a fire going near the wagon and tents pitched and Truitt was working on what smelled like a wonderful stew. He was clearly a cook, and had gotten excited over all the spices and staples Jimmy's mother had brought along.

Jimmy was surprised at how good horsemen Zach and Long were. Both clearly knew and loved the animals, and how to treat them with respect.

By the time the evening had ended, Jimmy was feeling great about his decision. And he really liked being around them. They were all very different, but all of them were on their own and they all knew that they had a better chance of getting west if they worked together.

The next morning, with Long and Truitt watching the wagon while hundreds of other wagons around it were pulling out, Jimmy and Zach and C.J. headed back into town to help Jimmy move Luke to his room in a three-story hotel that smelled of perfume and baking bread.

Jimmy paid for an entire month of room and food. Twelve dollars. The hotel owner was pleased to see the money up-front and promised to help Luke as much as he could, especially with Doc Davis looking out for him as well.

It turned out that Jimmy had needed the help moving Luke. Luke was so weak, he could barely walk, and climbing the long staircase from the hotel's big lobby to his second floor hotel room tired him so much, he fell asleep almost at once after he got into bed.

"That's normal," Doc Davis told the three of them in the narrow hallway outside of Luke's room. "I have arranged for two meals a day to be sent up to his room, and his bed pan emptied. I doubt he's going to be making it out too much for some time. I'll check him every day as well."

"Thanks, Doc," Jimmy said. "Very much appreciated."

"Just take care of yourself as well," Doc Davis said. "Stay dry and don't go getting chilled. You don't want to be in there on a cot with your brother, do you?"

"Not a chance, sir," Jimmy said.

After Doc left, Zach asked Jimmy, "You want to sit with your brother a while?"

Jimmy shook his head. He didn't need to do that. Luke was as well taken care of as anyone could be at this point. He just had to rest and get better.

"Then let's go see if we can find Benson," Zach said. "We have a gold mine deed to get back."

For the first time in what seemed like a long time, Jimmy felt as if his life was actually moving forward. And even though it was starting to rain slightly again, he was smiling.

They had no luck that day finding Benson, and after checking in with Luke, they headed back to the wagon, where Truitt had cooked an amazing meal of bread and stew.

Long, in the meantime, had brushed the two horses left there and checked them over for any problems. He had also fixed part of the tongue on the wagon that had cracked while crossing the last stream outside of Independence. He had also helped the Taskers with a repair before they pulled out.

It seemed to Jimmy that every one of them had a special skill that fit well with the other's skills. And Jimmy had no doubt he was just beginning to see all their special talents.

★ PART NINE ★
A PLAN

IT WAS FINALLY, ON THE fourth afternoon that the five of them were together, that Zach came back with news about Benson from a small hotel and saloon on the edge of town.

And it wasn't good news.

It seemed that Benson had been there for a week or so, camping out west of town and drinking every night with three or four friends.

"Is he still there?" C.J. asked.

"Nope," Zach said. "The sheriff chased Benson and his friends out of town. It seems they robbed an elderly couple."

"Any idea where he might be heading?" Jimmy asked.

Somehow, in the days since reaching Independence, Jimmy realized he had gone from being the scared kid hiding out from the killer of his parents to a person who wanted to track the killer and make him pay. He wasn't sure when that change had happened, but it sure had. And now, after getting this close to the killer, Jimmy didn't want to lose him now.

"From what the bartender I talked to told me," Zach said, "Benson was bragging that he had a gold mine deed in California and was headed there to work it."

"My father's mine," Jimmy said. He could feel his anger boiling, and right now all he wanted to do was hit something. But instead he forced himself to take a deep breath and try to think.

"I'm afraid it probably is," Zach said.

"How far of a head start does he have on us?" C.J. asked, clearly puzzling out what to do next as well.

"Three days," Zach said. "He left at the same time as those two big trains."

"More people to rob and kill along the way," Jimmy said.

The others just nodded at that.

"I'll meet you all back at camp," Jimmy said, feeling just about as low as he had felt in a week. "I need to tell Luke what we found out. We'll talk about what to do tonight over dinner."

A few minutes later, Jimmy turned into Doc Davis's office.

"Everything all right with Luke?" Doc asked

"Far as I know," Jimmy said. "I'm just headed there now, but I have a question to ask you. How long you think it will be until Luke will be able to travel?"

"West?" Doc Davis asked.

Jimmy nodded.

"At least two months, maybe more to be really safe," Doc said. "Or maybe not this year at all. It depends on how fast he recovers."

"Thanks, Doc," Jimmy said and left without another word. He had known that, but he needed the Doc to confirm it. Now he had no idea what they were going to do.

He was feeling sick to his stomach, not because he was now safe from the man who had killed his parents, but because it looked like that man was never going to pay for what he did.

By the middle of the summer, who knew where Benson would be. It had been hard enough finding him in a town the size of Independence. With the entire west to search, it would be impossible.

Luke was sitting up in bed, sipping on some soup, and he seemed to be stronger.

"Hi, little brother."

Jimmy didn't say anything, just pulled a chair over closer to Luke's bed and sat down.

Luke stared at him, frowning, then said, "You found Benson, didn't you? I'm ready to talk to the sheriff."

"Not really," Jimmy said. "He and his gang of killers were chased out of town three days ago, heading west, bragging that they had a mine to work in California."

Luke sighed and put the soup on the nightstand. "I was afraid of that. I've been laying here the last few days thinking about what to do if you did find him, or if he had left. I've got a plan."

Jimmy felt a sense of relief. His mother always said that Luke was the thinker between the two of them. Jimmy was the one who rushed in for the adventure.

"Do you trust the boys you met here?" Luke asked.

"I trust them," Jimmy said, nodding. "They've been helping me guard the wagon and it was Zach who found out where Benson went."

"Do they all want to go west?" Luke asked.

Jimmy nodded. "All of them do."

"Sell the wagon and all the equipment," Luke said, his voice firm and in control. "You'll never catch him with a wagon."

"Catch him!" Jimmy shouted. "I'm not leaving you!"

He pushed his chair back and stood. His stomach was clamped into a knot. No way could he leave Luke.

41

Luke held up his hand and kept talking, his voice level. "Let me finish. You need to buy three more horses and leave me one in the stable here. And leave me enough money to pay for a year of this room and board and Doc Davis and a little extra. The other two horses will carry supplies for you. Then the five of you head out to track Benson."

"No," Jimmy said firmly. "That's not a plan. I'm not leaving you."

"Jimmy, you know Doc Davis won't let me travel. And if I try, I'm going to be dead in two weeks. You just keep track of him, don't show yourself, and I'll meet you in Sacramento next July 4th. Then we'll deal with that killer together. It's the only way we can make him pay for what he did to Mother and Father."

Jimmy just shook his head and said nothing. He hated this idea.

"You can't help me by sitting here, you know that?" Luke said, staring at Jimmy. "You did a great job getting me to Doc Davis on your own. You also have to know I believe in you to even suggest that my little brother travel clear out west without me?"

Jimmy nodded. "But I can't lose you."

Luke laughed and patted the bed. "I'll be right here. We'll only be apart until next summer."

Jimmy said nothing. The idea of going west alone terrified him more than he wanted to admit.

More than facing Benson, actually.

"Besides," Luke said, smiling, "You've got your friends to help out, and I've got Doc Davis's daughter to keep me company. Better than your ugly face."

"I can't argue with that," Jimmy said, managing a smile.

"Think about it," Luke said. "But you know I'm right. You have to go, at least to keep track of Benson until I can help you get that killer to justice."

Luke scooted down in the bed and closed his eyes with a sigh. "I envy you the adventure, little brother."

"When you're well, we'll have adventures together," Jimmy said.

"You have a deal," Luke said. "Now get out of here so I can get some sleep. And get a good price for the wagon and the equipment. Make Father proud."

Jimmy left, pulling the door tight behind him.

By the time he had finished a very slow ride out to the wagon, he knew that Luke was right.

There was no choice.

To stop Benson, or even keep track of him, Jimmy and his new friends had to go and go soon.

They had to chase Benson into the wilderness.

⋆ PART TEN ⋆
HEADED WEST AGAIN

JIMMY FINALLY GOT HIS WISH to see a buffalo ten days out of Independence. It was May 7th.

It had taken two days for the five of them to sell the wagon and equipment and buy three more horses. During the first days on the trail, Long had pointed out some plants that were poison, and others that were good to eat. It seemed to Jimmy that there was a lot to learn about Long. And he had a lot to teach them about survival in the west.

Before they left, Jimmy had paid for three months in advance for Luke's hotel room and food, and gave Doc Davis another payment for his services. Then he gave some money to Luke, enough for Luke to pay for a year in the hotel and supplies to get west next spring.

Jimmy had left a few of the family's most personal things with Luke in the hotel room, and had given his father's rifle to Zach. He seemed to be the only one of them who wanted to touch it. Jimmy said it would come in handy for hunting. Everything else, Jimmy sold to buy camping gear and supplies that they packed on the extra horses and in their own saddlebags.

After all that, he didn't have much money left, but he didn't tell anyone but Zach.

The goodbye with Luke had been hard for Jimmy, but after a few days on the trail, Jimmy's mood had lightened and he had started looking forward to the adventure ahead.

On Long's suggestion, they didn't push the horses, but instead just walked them along at a steady pace, often between wagons in the long trains. Jimmy had figured that Benson was only five or six days ahead by the time they left Independence. Considering the eighteen different legs of the trip that lay between Independence and Sacramento, and how far they all had to travel, that wasn't very far.

Zach had said that since Benson and his men didn't have any money when they were chased out of town, more than likely they would join onto a train to find food and rob some unsuspecting family.

So each night, they camped near a different train camp, not only for protection, but to get to know those in the train to make sure Benson wasn't among them. The last thing they wanted to do was pass him without knowing it.

For the first leg, which was about a hundred miles from Independence to the Kansas River ferry, the trail was packed with wagons and people walking. At times, the trail seemed more like a busy city street than the main wagon road west.

But on the second leg, a two hundred mile stretch northwest across grasslands to the Platte River, the wagons seemed to spread out some, even inside the same train. It usually took a wagon about two weeks to make that leg, but they made it in six days, traveling at a steady pace, passing wagon after wagon, all with friendly faces waving at them as they went by.

Jimmy was starting to get a better idea of the vastness of the country. As far as the eye could see, it was green grasslands and low hills. The air was clean and fresh, especially after a rain. The only real excitement they encountered during the first days out of Independence was getting across a couple of swollen streams. It was clear that wagons had been lost in those streambeds, from the looks of the ruined equipment scattered downstream. Some family's dreams hadn't lasted very long.

When they reached the South Fork of the Platte River, the trail turned back westward and followed the south bank. The river was wide and brown and seemed to flow slowly and gently along. By this third leg of the trip, the wagons were really starting to spread out more and more, and sometimes it was impossible to tell where one company ended and another started. And there were more and more travelers in groups of two or three wagons, easy pickings for a man like Benson.

At one point, C.J. asked Long about Indians in this area. Long had pointed to the north. "Pawnee territory. To the south is Cheyenne. We're moving between them, so no problems."

Jimmy was glad to hear that, and glad even more that Long was with them. Not only did he know where the Indian territories were, but he had found some great roots that Truitt had used in some wonderful tasting stews.

The next morning, Long pointed at a dried brown pile to one side of the trail. "Fuel for a fire," he said. "Buffalo chips."

That had gotten them all excited and searching along the rolling hills around the river for any signs of actual buffalo. But they didn't see any that day. However, Long was correct about the dried chips being great fuel for the campfire.

Finally, on the tenth day out of Independence, a man from one of the wagon trains they were slowly passing came riding hard and fast back toward his wagon from a ridge to the south. "Buffalo!" he shouted when he got close enough.

The cry went up and down the wagon train like a brush fire.

"Looks like we might be eating meat tonight," Truitt had said, smiling at Jimmy.

Jimmy was so excited, he could hardly keep his heart from beating right out of his chest,

"Can a rifle like this stop one?" Zach asked Long, pointing to Jimmy's father's rifle tied to his saddlebag.

"In the heart, right behind the front legs," Long said. "Two or three shots, maybe. But don't shoot a bull. The meat is too tough. A small cow is the best."

Zach nodded.

Then Long turned to Jimmy. "I will camp below that rock ledge with the packhorses until you return."

"Not interested in seeing a buffalo?" C.J. asked.

"I have seen far too many of them," Long said, then took the pack-horses and moved slowly off toward the rocks.

"Let's go find some buffalo," Jimmy said, smiling at his friends.

With that, they headed at full ride toward the hill where the man had come from. Two other men were right ahead of them, and Jimmy had no doubt many others from the train would be following.

As they crested over the rise, at first Jimmy couldn't see anything different. Then it dawned on him that part of the shallow valley to his right was covered in brown instead of waving green grass.

Buffalo!

What looked to be thousands of them. The stories were right. It did look like a sea of buffalo.

"Oh, my," Truitt said, awe in his voice.

Jimmy just stared. The buffalo were majestic creatures. Jimmy could see a number of larger bulls, and hundreds of smaller calves, grazing near their mothers. Even from a distance, he could tell they were bigger than any cattle he had ever seen. The bulls looked to be almost as big as their horses, not as tall but much wider.

A half dozen men rode past them, heading for the buffalo, rifles out and ready.

Jimmy glanced over at Zach. "Think you might be able to down one of those?"

Zach looked stunned, but then he smiled and nodded. "My dad said I was the best shot he had ever seen. I just have to get close enough."

"Let's go," Jimmy said. "C.J., Truitt, we'll try to cut out a small cow from the herd, let Zach get a clean shot."

"Right with you," C.J. said.

With that, Jimmy spurred his horse into motion down the hill toward the herd, following the men from the train. His heart was racing and he was having trouble catching his breath. Never, in all his life in Boston, did he think he would ever be doing something like this. What would his friends back there think if they could see him?

What would Luke think?

The buffalo were spooked by the men riding at them, and turned to run, in mass. The sound was almost deafening, louder than a train pulling into a station. And even on the horse, Jimmy could feel the ground shaking from that many large animals running at once.

Jimmy led them to the right, while the other men went to the left side of the herd. He had his eye on one medium-sized cow that was on the edge of the herd. He pointed at it and beside him Truitt shouted, "Got it, boss!"

Then C.J., seemingly completely fearless, did something that Jimmy would have never thought of doing. He took his horse into the herd, running with it, trying to cut the cow farther away from the herd.

It seemed to be working until suddenly shots echoed through the air from the other side of the herd.

The buffalo got even more frantic, running faster and harder.

And the entire herd turned toward them.

Jimmy found himself and his horse surrounded by buffalo, all running at top speed. He and his horse had no choice but to run with the herd.

He didn't dare stop.

He tried to ease his horse sideways, but there was no place to go. He was completely penned in by stampeding buffalo that smashed against his legs and his horse.

It was like riding while the ground around him was moving at the same time.

To his left, C.J. was stuck as well, a look of total concentration on his face as he tried to keep his horse on its feet. Jimmy couldn't see either Truitt or Zach, and hoped they were out of the herd and behind them.

"Ease back!" Jimmy shouted at C.J., pulling his horse back just enough to slow him, but not turn him. He didn't dare try to stop fast or turn. In the thundering of the herd, he could barely hear his own yell.

As he slowed just a little, the buffalo started moving around him, running forward, opening up spaces as the herd started to pass him.

C.J. glanced over and saw what Jimmy was doing, then started to do the same thing.

It seemed to take forever for the herd to pass Jimmy completely, but actually it must have only been a few seconds. As he made it into the open behind the herd, he let out the breath he must have been holding. He was sweating and his heart was beating so hard, it felt like it might explode.

If his horse had gone down in that herd, he would have died a horrible death.

He glanced around. Zach and Truitt were following a distance back, looks of worry on both of their faces.

The herd passed C.J. and the four of them stopped and tried to catch their breaths.

"I thought you two were dead for sure," Truitt said, shaking his head and laughing.

"I thought we were too," Jimmy said. He held his hands on his pants legs so that the others wouldn't see them shaking.

"Let's not do that again," C.J. said, sweat pouring down his face. He took off his glasses and tried to clean them, but his hands were shaking too much, so he gave up. "I think next time, I'll just stay with Long and the horses."

"Great buffalo hunters we are, huh?" Zach said, then he laughed. After a moment, all four of them were laughing.

Jimmy was just glad that all four of them were still alive so that they could laugh.

★ PART ELEVEN ★
A REAL HUNT

SINCE THEIR FIRST EXPERIENCE WITH buffalo, they had seen a half dozen other herds before reaching the South Fork crossing. Some of the herds were smaller, some closer to the trail. But Jimmy's great desire to see them had worn off completely. He now had a huge respect for the big creatures.

After spotting the third herd, Long had finally agreed, after much pushing from Zach and Truitt, to help them to get some meat for dinner. As far as C.J. was concerned, he never wanted to see a buffalo again and he said he would be glad to watch the horses.

Long showed Zach a rock to sit behind with the rifle just down a shallow valley from the herd. "Shoot a small cow or large calf as it runs past. That will be more meat than we can carry."

Zach had nodded and looked worried when Long took his horse away, walking it slowly back to let C.J. hold it.

Then Long told Jimmy to go to the left of the herd, Truitt to the right, and he said he would stay directly behind them. "We move up to them slowly," Long said, "then when I give the signal, wave your hat and shout."

"We'll drive them directly at Zach," Jimmy said, glancing down the valley ahead of the herd where Zach crouched behind a rock.

"The beasts will turn slightly left, following the valley, and will pass beside Zach's position," Long said. "They are lazy creatures by nature and will not run up a hill unless they are forced to."

Jimmy just hoped, for Zach's sake, Long was right about that.

A few minutes later, they were all in position and Long gave the signal. This time, Jimmy had no plan on getting too close to the herd, and he noticed that Truitt stayed a safe distance away as well.

The herd of large beasts rumbled into motion, moving toward Zach. Again, Jimmy couldn't believe the noise and how much the ground shook.

For a moment, Jimmy thought Long was going to be wrong and Zach was going to have to depend on hiding behind a rock to save his life. But then, as Long had said they would, the herd turned left, giving Zach a clear and close shot at the nearest creatures.

Zach leveled the rifle on one small cow and fired twice.

The cow went nose down, tumbled once, and then lay there, not moving.

Long motioned for C.J. to bring Zach's horse and the packhorses, and all of them moved toward the dead buffalo.

Jimmy was amazed at how ugly the creature was up close. And Long had been right, they were very smelly beasts, like a rancid stew left out in the sun for too many days. Their hair was patchy and bugs crawled all over them.

Long gave Jimmy, Truitt, and Zach step-by-step instructions on how to get the meat out of the beast, how to pack it, and so on. By the time they were finished, all three of them had to take a swim in the cold brown water of the river just to get the smell off.

But that night, the buffalo steaks that Truitt cooked were wonderful. Jimmy figured it was almost worth it.

Almost.

★ PART TWELVE ★
A BIG STORM

THE NEXT AFTERNOON THEY REACHED the South Fork Crossing. All Jimmy could think about was that it wasn't possible to cross that wide a river. It had to be at least a half-mile across. It looked more like a lake than a river. He could swim, but not that good.

"We're going across that?" Truitt asked.

"All of them are," Jimmy said, pointing at the two hundred wagons that were camped along the banks of the river. "We can make it."

"I'm not much of a swimmer," Truitt said, clearly not happy with the idea.

"Neither am I," C.J. said.

"Your horse can swim," Long said. "Just stay in the saddle."

Truitt looked at Long. "Oh, sure, easy for you to say."

As the five of them sat and stared at the ford from the high bank, at least twenty wagons were in the water at one point or another in the crossing. And more were camped on the other side.

From what Jimmy could tell, none of the wagons seemed to be in too far over their beds, and none of the horses seemed to be swimming. That, at least, was a good sign.

They spent the rest of that day camped with the wagons, making sure Benson wasn't among those waiting to cross. Then, the next morning, they went into the water.

As Jimmy pushed his horse gently into the slowly moving river, he wasn't sure what was more frightening, riding in a herd of buffalo or crossing a river a half-mile wide. At that moment, he almost wished he was back with the buffalo.

But the river turned out to be shallow all the way across, and he didn't even get his boots wet. That afternoon, after checking the wagons camped on the other side for any sign of Benson, they headed away from the river into the fourth leg of the long trip.

From what C.J. told them, it was just over one hundred and eighty miles from the crossing to Fort Laramie. More than likely, that would be where they would catch up to Benson.

The trail from the crossing cut across a shallow range of hills and started up the North Fork of the Platte River.

The hills around them now were rocky and higher, and the brush thinner. And by this point, the wagons were really spread out. Sometimes they would ride for a few hours before catching up to a stopped band of wagons.

"We're in Sioux territory," Long said on the third day. "We should camp at night with a wagon company for safety."

Jimmy had no argument with that.

Jimmy wanted to ask Long many questions about his mother's people, but figured now wouldn't be the time. Maybe later in the trip. Right now, Long looked very serious and focused on the rocks and hills around them and Jimmy let him concentrate.

On the third evening as they were moving along the river, it seemed as if the sky around them and above the mountains just suddenly turned a pitch black. It had rained off and on for the entire trip, but no storm before had looked this bad.

Zach pointed at the coming clouds. "I think we need to take cover."

"I agree," Long said. "That will have some strong winds and lightning with those clouds."

"How about up that canyon there?" Truitt pointed to a rock-lined canyon "We should be able to anchor our tents pretty well there."

"It's not with a wagon company," Jimmy said. He didn't much like the looks of the coming clouds either, but he also didn't like the idea of camping alone in Sioux territory without a lot of people around them. And at the moment, there was no wagon company within sight along the trail.

"The Sioux will take cover as well," Long said. "They consider a storm like this one bad medicine."

"Can't argue with them there," Truitt said as a rumbling of thunder echoed out over the river.

With one more look at the clouds, Jimmy said, "Let's move before we get soaked."

At a full gallop, they turned away from the trail and headed up the rocky canyon, following a shallow stream. There were numbers of side canyons off the main one, but Long led them to what seemed like an alcove water had cut into the rock. The walls of the canyon would shelter them both from most of the wind and the lightning.

They secured the horses, then madly worked to pitch and secure their tents. Jimmy had just finished and crawled inside when the first gust of wind really rocked his tent and a moment later the rains started.

Chances are, it was going to be a very long night.

He must have dozed because the next thing he realized, lightning and thunder were shaking the ground around him, and water was pouring into his tent.

He grabbed his saddlebags and got out into the storm quickly. In one flash of lightning, he saw that the small stream they had camped beside was quickly rising.

"Water!" he shouted. "Everybody up and out!"

Another very close strike of lightning spooked the horses and he barely got to them in time to hold them from trying to break away.

"We need to get out of this canyon!" Long shouted over the thundering of the storm.

"And fast!" Jimmy shouted.

He could only see the others through the pitch black pouring rain when lightning lit up the canyon. But from what he could see, the others were scrambling to gather up their gear and get to the horses.

The water around them was coming up faster than Jimmy could have imagined possible. He decided to leave his tent and bedroll. He doubted he could get to them in the rising water anyway.

He managed to get a saddle on his horse while the others worked frantically in the pouring rain beside him. By the time he got the gear on one of the packhorses and got mounted, the water had risen so fast, it was up to his waist.

Somehow, he got his horse and the packhorse headed downstream, but now both horses seemed to be swimming in the strong current and it was everything Jimmy could do to just hang on.

A lightning strike showed a side canyon ahead that looked mostly dry. He tried to turn his horse in that direction, and somehow the horse got footing and pulled out of the water, with the packhorse following.

Lightning strikes, one right after another, gave him just enough light in the rain to work his way up the canyon to a high, wide shelf area that would be above any flooding.

There he dismounted and tried to hold the horses as tight as he could against the shelter of the rock wall.

The rain pounded on him as he knelt down. He was so cold, he was shivering and his fingers were numb.

Around him, the storm raged, as if the Earth itself was mad at him.

He stayed pressed against the rocks, trying to hold the horses from bolting with every close lightning strike and thunderous clap.

None of the others had made it into this side canyon.

More than likely, they had been swept downstream and into the big river and were dead. Even if they could swim, no one could survive that swirling torrent in the rock canyon for very long.

It was going to be a very long night.

He had lost his friends.

Mother Nature and the west had clearly won this battle.

And again, he was completely alone.

★ PART THIRTEEN ★
ALONE AGAIN

THE MORNING LIGHT WAS BARELY allowing Jimmy to see the narrow side canyon around him. The air was bitingly cold, and Jimmy was soaking wet from the long night in the rain. He needed to get dry and warm quickly, before he got sick. He knew, without a doubt, that this kind of cold and wet could kill a man out here in the wilderness faster than any wild animal.

Faster than a killer like Benson.

Jimmy had to get dry and warm up as soon as he could, somehow.

In the faint light, he slowly eased himself and his two horses down off the rock ledge he had reached during the flood. The canyon was no more than a hundred paces across and the walls were as tall as three Boston banks. The stream flowing through the bottom of the canyon now was only a fast torrent, not at all dangerous-looking. But he could see the watermarks up the rock walls where the water had been last night in the flash flood. He had been lucky to survive. He had no idea how the rest of them could have.

Yesterday, there had been an easy path through the rocks. Now the way down to the main canyon and the wagon trail was completely blocked by boulders and brush and walls of mud. In one place, the water was flowing under some boulders that were far too big to get a horse over. It was clear he wasn't getting down the canyon and back to the river that way, at least not with two horses. He was going to need to find another way out.

He took a deep breath and shouted, "Zach! Long!"

His shout echoed among the rocks and then died under the sounds of the stream.

Nothing.

No one shouted back.

He had to keep believing they were alive. He had lost his parents, and left his sick brother Luke in Independence. He couldn't lose his friends as well. He had to find them.

Or at least find their bodies.

He shivered and felt light-headed. The cold and wet was clearly getting to him. He had to keep moving, find a way to get dry.

He headed back up the side canyon, sometimes wading in deep mud, other times climbing over rocks, looking for any trail up and over the steep rock walls. Finally he found a path that he could get the horses up to a ridgeline and then work his way around and back down to the river.

At the top, in the morning sun, he stopped, took off his wet clothes and wrung the last of the cold water from them, letting the sun warm him as best it could so early in the day.

He had some mostly dry extra clothes in his saddlebag, so he put those on, then put on his light coat, and then put back on his heaviest coat. He would be sweating this way soon enough, but that was what he needed to do to get warm.

An hour later, as the warmth of the sun had him warmed back to normal, he headed back down into the wide valley that ran along the side of the North Fork of the Platte River. It took him almost three hours to go the few miles down to the trail, the riding was so rough.

No wagon companies were in sight in either direction. With one look at the wagon trail, Jimmy knew why. Every stream that flowed out of the hills above the river had flooded last night in the storm. And now the trail was cut with deep gashes, sometimes up to the height of ten men deep. Those streams would take time to work wagons through or around. The next company through here was basically going to have to build a lot of new trail.

The river itself flowed dark brown with mud and much higher than it had yesterday. There was all kind of debris floating in the river, and as Jimmy watched, the canvas top of one wagon floated past.

Jimmy rode back to the mouth of the canyon he had been trapped in, then on foot he searched the length of the huge gash in the ground from the canyon wall to the river's edge, looking for any signs of his friends.

Nothing.

More than likely, they had been swept into the river. Maybe a couple of them had made it out downstream.

He headed down the trail they had come up yesterday. The going was slow, as he had to pick his way over one washed-out gulley after another. But finally, he reached a half dozen men working out ahead of a wagon company, trying to find or build a new trail through the area.

Jimmy talked to all of them, asking if they had run across any boys about his age along the river.

"Nope," one man said. "Just a number of dead horses and cattle floating past. Sorry."

Jimmy sure hoped those horses were from a company cf wagons up the river farther. He didn't want to think about any of them being his friends' horses.

By the middle of the afternoon, he gave up his search and turned back west. He might as well go on to Fort Laramie. Maybe the rest of the group would be waiting for him there. More than likely, if they had searched for him and couldn't find him, that's what Zach would have them do.

They would be there. He had to believe that.

⋆ PART FOURTEEN ⋆
BENSON SHOWS UP

FINALLY, ALONE AND TIRED, JIMMY came face-to-face with the killer of his parents.

With the light just barely tinting the sky on the morning of the second day after the flash flood, Jimmy had worked his way into the settlement beside the military buildings of Fort Laramie. There were a large number of saloons spaced with even more general stores than Independence had. He knew the stores sold expensive supplies for those who needed them at this point of the trip west. This would be the last major re-supply stop until the west side of the Nevada Territory. Entire wagon trains full of supplies had left Independence ahead of the main rush of settlers to stock these stores.

The town was laid out on a gentle slope, and to one side were hundreds of Sioux Indians camped in groups of lodges. Long had told them that his people would be here, trading with the settlers, but Jimmy was still surprised to see that many camped that close to the town and the military buildings.

On the other side of the town were a good three hundred wagons filling a hillside and a wide valley. Smoke drifted lazily through the crisp, clear air from all the morning campfires.

Jimmy had rode into the mostly still-dark town, moving down the main street looking for any sign of his friends or their horses.

Nothing.

Luckily, he had saved what was left of his father's money when scrambling for safety in the flood. He needed a new tent and bedroll. He pulled his horses up to a general store that was just opening.

Suddenly, the man he hated the most walked out of the saloon right beside the store.

Jake Benson stood right there in front of Jimmy on the wooden sidewalk, not more than twenty paces away.

Jimmy sat in his saddle, stunned and frozen. That man had shot Jimmy's mother in the back. Jimmy could feel his anger building like a pot ready to boil. He wanted to run at Benson screaming and shouting and just beat the man to death with his fists, but he knew he wasn't big enough or strong enough to do that to Benson.

And besides, Benson had a gun and his men were with him.

"Just follow him until I can join you," his brother Luke had said. *"Then we will take care of him together."*

Jimmy made himself take a deep breath, then he dismounted and eased around to the other side of his horse so he was hidden from Benson. He had been lucky the killer hadn't spotted him.

Jimmy's hands were shaking, his breathing shallow and swift. Benson scared him to death, and made him fantastically angry at the same time.

Benson laughed at something another man coming out of the saloon said. Then Benson and his three men mounted up and started toward the edge of town, heading west. There was no sign of the man Luke had shot.

Jimmy mounted back up as well. Staying far enough back as to barely still see the four men in the distance, he rode along behind them.

An hour later, it was clear that Benson and his men were on the wagon trail, moving at a steady walking pace, following a company of wagons that had just pulled out.

Jimmy turned around. At least he knew where Benson was headed. West.

For a gold mine.

Now Jimmy had to find his friends. He could afford to wait around Fort Laramie for three or four days and still catch up with Benson. The killer and his men had had a five or six day head start on him out of Independence and Jimmy had caught him this time. He would catch the killer again, he had no doubt.

Jimmy couldn't let Luke and his parents down. He had to keep following Benson, even if he had to do it alone.

The sun was cresting over the hills as Jimmy got back into town and tied up his horses in front of a general store. As he was about to climb up onto the wooden sidewalk and go inside, he glanced down the street.

Zach!

Jimmy couldn't believe it. His best friend was standing against the wall of a saloon with his back to Jimmy. Zach was clearly watching the trail coming in from the east, the trail that Jimmy had come in on three hours earlier.

Jimmy wanted to shout and jump for joy. He couldn't believe Zach was still alive. He headed down the sidewalk with a smile on his face that hurt it was so big.

He walked up behind Zach and then said in his most serious voice, "Is Truitt working wagons again?"

Zach spun around, then, smiling, he grabbed Jimmy by the shoulders and shook him. "You're alive. I can't believe it. You're alive. C.J. said you would be."

"And you didn't believe him?" Jimmy asked, smiling just as hard.

"We searched that entire area, but we couldn't get back up the canyon, and by the time we went around to an area on top of the hills to look down into the canyon, there was no sign of you."

"We?" Jimmy asked. "Is everyone all right?"

Zach nodded, smiling. "Banged up a little, and the horses have some cuts and scrapes. That stream just dumped us out onto the bank of the river like so much garbage. Long has been taking care of the horses and they're going to be good as rain. But we lost some of our provisions and gear. We've been living on what's left of the buffalo meat, camped down near the wagons since yesterday."

"Well," Jimmy said, "Let's go get everyone. I think I have enough left of my father's money to get whatever new gear we need. I lost some of mine as well."

"You managed to save your father's money from the flood?" Zach asked.

"Sure did," Jimmy said, "and a packhorse."

Then Jimmy got serious. "This morning I saw Benson."

"Where?" Zach asked, clearly stunned. "What did you do?"

Jimmy patted his best friend on the shoulder. "Let's head back to the camp. I'll tell everything over breakfast. We have plans to make and a gold mine to get back."

Zach laughed. "Oh, I can't tell you how much I love the sound of that."

"Yeah, me too," Jimmy said. "Me too."

★ PART FIFTEEN ★
A NEW TEAM MEMBER

WITH LONG TENDING TO THE slightly injured horses, the four of them went back into town that afternoon to get supplies for the trip west. It was going to take every dime of the money Jimmy had left to re-supply, especially in Fort Laramie.

As Jimmy was helping Truitt and C.J. carry gear out of one store, he came out to find Zach, who had been guarding the horses, sitting on the edge of the wooden sidewalk next to a young man who looked to be around Jimmy's age of twenty. The man was writing in a notebook. He had on a tall black hat and his long dark hair flowed out from under the back of the hat.

Across the street, two drunks were taking wild swings at each other and then falling into the mud. As Jimmy watched, the guy seemed to be writing down what he was seeing, stumble-by-stumble, blow-by-missed-blow.

Zach glanced up to see Jimmy watching.

"Meet Joshua Mark," Zach said. "Future journalist and storyteller."

"Call me Josh," the man said, glancing up at Jimmy. "You two got separated in the big storm, didn't you?"

Jimmy glanced at Zach, who shrugged. "I didn't tell him."

"Saw your meeting this morning," Josh said, still writing down what was happening with the two drunks across the street. "Figured it out for myself."

"Pretty sharp," Jimmy said, surprised. "You with one of the wagon companies?"

"Nope," Josh said. "I'm just trying to head out west. I'm going to be like Mark Twain and write down stories about the west and then sell them."

Jimmy stared at the side of Josh's face as he wrote down how the fight had ended, with one drunk falling against a horse rail and knocking himself out. This guy was clearly very, very smart. Jimmy had had a number of years in school, but he couldn't write anywhere near as well or as fast as Josh was doing.

"Who's this?" C.J. asked as he came out of the store and dropped down on the edge of the wooden sidewalk beside Josh.

He noticed what Josh had been doing and said, "Hey, can I read it?"

"Sure," Josh said, handing C.J. the pages held together with a strip of leather. Josh pointed to a place on one page and said, "Start there."

"You have family?" Jimmy asked, starting to like this guy more and more every second. He was clearly very smart, maybe even smarter than C.J., if that was possible. And they were going to need smart if they were to do anything with Benson when they caught up with him again.

"Nope," Josh said. "Just me. Parents died, no one else."

"You got a horse?" Zach asked.

"Nope," Josh said. "I was just going to walk along with one of the trains, maybe work for some food along the way when I could. That's how I got this far."

Jimmy motioned that Zach should follow him back into the general store. As Zach stood, C.J. said, "This is really good. You have more like it?"

"I sure do," Josh said, smiling.

Inside the store, Jimmy turned to Zach. "Are you thinking what I'm thinking?"

"We're headed into some really rough country," Zach said. "We're better off if there's more of us riding together."

"And the mine?" Jimmy asked.

"I have a hunch," Zach said, smiling, "that there's going to be more than enough work and gold for all of us."

"I agree," Jimmy said, thinking about what it would take for Josh to join them. He likely had his own gear, and they had an extra horse. They only needed one packhorse.

Jimmy looked at Zach. "Let's ask him if he is interested in joining us."

"Who's going to join us?" Truitt asked, coming up with a handful of spices in cloth bags and a block of salt.

"The man outside with the tall black hat," Zach said. "He's as sharp as a drapery tack."

"The guy doing the writing?" Truitt asked, glancing out the front door.

Jimmy nodded, looking for any sign that Truitt might not like the idea.

"Great by me," Truitt said, turning around to go back to shopping. "I have a hunch that where we are heading, we're going to need all the help we can get."

Jimmy laughed. "That settles it, then. Three votes win."

Zach pointed back out the door at how C.J. and Josh were laughing over something. "I'm betting you'll get a fourth vote real easy."

That night, around a warm campfire of buffalo chips, Truitt cooked them a great meal and the six friends talked late into the darkness.

By the end of the evening, Jimmy was very glad they had met Josh.

By mid-morning of the next day, they were headed west.

Four of the eighteen legs to reach California were behind them. The easy four.

⋆ PART SIXTEEN ⋆
THEY MAKE HARD PROGRESS

THE VASTNESS OF THE WEST was overwhelming to Jimmy, not in a bad way, but with a feeling that kept generating excitement. Every day he marveled at one sight or another, from small things like the sight of an animal he had never seen to stunning rock formations.

And the smells seemed to constantly change, from dry sagebrush to wetlands along the river.

They had traveled through the fifth leg up the river to the ford of the North Fork of the Platte River, making a steady pace for seven days. The trail was much, much rougher, and the wagon companies were clearly having more trouble with the pull.

They were doing fine, walking most of the time to rest the horses.

In a couple places, the trail was a full day's ride away from the river, so they had to watch their water more carefully.

At Independence Rock, all of them carved their names on the rock, along with thousands of other names. Jimmy couldn't believe so many people had gone past this place.

This was a rough trip for even someone in as good of shape as he was. And it was clear that if his brother had tried to make even these early legs, it would have killed him.

The seventh leg took them up to the top of the South Pass and over the Continental Divide. The air, the higher they climbed, got colder at nights, and twice over the four days up to the pass, it snowed on them during the night.

They walked the horses even more, and moved shorter distances because none of them were used to the higher altitude. Jimmy found it amazing that all the mountains around them were still covered in white.

He had never seen anything so beautiful in all his life. Pictures and paintings just didn't do it justice in any fashion.

And the smell of the pine in the crisp morning air just made his head spin in happiness.

The main trail then angled north to Fort Hall , then back south to the split in the Oregon and California Trails forty miles to the south of Fort Hall.

Fort Hall was small, with few saloons or general stores. Considering that it was a major spot on the trip, it wasn't much to see.

There were a few Snake Indians camped near town, and very few wagons. It was the last place to really buy supplies on either the California or Oregon Trails, but most wagons didn't need anything here and just camped for a night, then pressed on.

"We're about halfway to California from Independence," C.J. said in the morning as they rode out of Fort Hall.

"The easy half," Josh said.

Jimmy didn't like the sound of that at all.

Forty miles later, they reached Raft River, where the Oregon Trail split from the California Trail.

The southern California trail went along the Raft River for a while, then went up and over a few ranges until finally dropping down on Goose Creek.

It was on June 14th, as they worked their way along a small stream called Goose Creek, just inside the eastern edge of Nevada, the union's newest state, that everything changed.

The trail ahead went around a low ridge and it was from that direction that the sounds of gunfire came.

Close, very close.

Then a woman screamed.

Jimmy froze, wondering if that was what his mother had sounded like when Benson killed his father.

Then there were more shots and another scream.

"Get down!" Zach shouted.

All the boys dove from their horses and scrambled for cover in a small grove of trees near the spring.

Jimmy had no idea what was happening, but it didn't sound good.

Again, the woman screamed loud and long.

All Jimmy could think about was that they had to do something to help her.

Anything.

His mother hadn't had anyone to help her.

The woman's next scream echoed over the hills and then died out in a horrible way with one more shot.

Too late to help her. That was all he could think.

Jimmy glanced around at his five friends. What had they gotten into this time?

⋆ PART SEVENTEEN ⋆
DEATH COMES TO THE WEST

THE WOMAN'S SCREAMS WERE FRIGHTENING in how sharp and clear they carried over the wide Goose Creek valley.

Jimmy jerked around in the saddle of his horse, trying to figure out where the shots and screams were coming from as Long, who had been leading the six of them at a steady pace, immediately dismounted and pulled his horse toward a grove of tall trees beside the stream.

Jimmy did the same, realizing just how big a target he was sitting up there on the horse.

So far, the vastness of the West had scared and overwhelmed him, a flash flood had almost killed him, and he had barely escaped being trampled by a buffalo herd. Yet that woman's scream sent more chills through his blood than anything he had heard since leaving Independence.

Around him, the Goose Creek valley looked like a peaceful place, a wonderful green strip of life in the otherwise brown hills. Large leafy trees bordered the creek, and kept the area cool from the heat of the day.

Keeping his head low, Jimmy followed Long deeper into the trees, finally stopping and tying up his horse on a large log.

All six then hunkered down together, listening. Not even a slight breeze broke the silence of the valley and the gentle sounds of the stream. Jimmy could hear his own heart pounding in his chest and he tried not to pant too loudly.

Two more shots rang out over the trees.

Jimmy could only think about what had happened to his mother, how she must have screamed when Jake Benson shot his father in the back. Jimmy wondered if his mother's screams sounded as chilling before she was shot as well.

The scream came again, then another few shots. Finally, the valley settled into an uneasy silence.

Like the silence at a funeral.

Jimmy pushed the thought away and turned to Long and the rest of his friends. Long knew the West and distances and seemingly everything else about survival out in the wilderness. Jimmy had come to count on him and his special talents.

"Indians?" Jimmy asked, his voice barely above a whisper.

He forced himself to breathe and try to keep calm, not let his total hate of guns and the sound of those screams get in his way.

"Bannocks in this area," Long said, nodding, his long black hair flowing around his shoulders. "They are a mean group."

Josh, their newest member, shook his head, his notebook and pen clutched tightly in his hand. "That doesn't sound like the type of guns the Bannocks would have."

All five of them turned to stare at their newest member. Clearly, besides writing stories, Josh knew guns. That was a talent that Jimmy would have to keep in mind in the future.

Long nodded, then whispered. "Josh is right. We need to take a look."

"Can you tell where the sounds are coming from?" Zach asked. His hands squeezed their only gun, a hunting rifle that used to belong to Jimmy' father.

Jimmy could tell that the sounds of the woman screaming had bothered Zach a lot as well. Usually Zach was the calm one. Now he was squeezing the butt of the rifle like it was a dishtowel he was trying to wring water out of.

"Just over the ridge to the right," Long said and Josh nodded in agreement.

Jimmy glanced at Josh. "Can you tell how many differen: guns were fired?"

"Three," Josh said. "One rifle, two revolvers."

Even Long looked impressed.

"Glad you're along with us," Truitt said, patting Josh's shoulder.

Josh smiled and nodded thanks.

Jimmy glanced around at his five friends and decided they needed to act. This was the west, after all.

"Truitt, you and C.J. stay with the horses. Be saddled up and ready to come riding fast with all of them if we shout for help."

Truitt nodded.

Zach checked quickly to make sure the rifle was fully loaded. Between blood-thirsty outlaws, stampeding buffalo, and deadly weather, the West was proving itself to be no parlor game.

"Go slow and stay quiet," Long said softly as he headed out for the small rise to the right of the stream.

To Jimmy, it seemed to take them forever to get to the top of that hill, picking their way first through the trees, then up the gentle incline through the sagebrush, moving slowly and carefully, staying in behind Long.

But in reality, it couldn't have been longer than a minute.

Just before they reached the top, the crackling of a large fire could be heard from the other side, then a man laughing.

The sound made Jimmy catch his breath.

It was the sound of evil. Pure evil.

Long motioned for them to spread out beside him, and then they crawled the last few feet on hands and knees to the top of the ridge as the hot sun beat down on their backs.

Beyond the top of the hill, Goose Creek doubled back into the sheltered alcove of a small valley. The main trail stayed in the larger valley. In the shelter between the two ridges, someone had built a small ranch with a slanted-roof barn and a cabin. A garden had been planted beyond the cabin, and behind the farm was a large grove of trees, so thick that Jimmy could barely see down through them. It looked like a wonderful oasis in the vast desert and rough lands of the Wyoming Territory.

The house was starting to burn, black smoke billowing up into the clear morning sky. The crackling of the flames was getting louder as more and more of the house caught fire. Sparks flew into the air before vanishing.

And there were three bodies scattered around the burning building.

Jimmy was stunned and sick to his stomach at what he saw. Clearly the family that had lived in the house had been shot down.

Four horses were tied up near the barn right below them, and the sounds of men talking came from the barn.

Jimmy looked at the horses. He knew one of them.

Benson!

The man who had killed Jimmy's parents had now killed another family.

★ PART EIGHTEEN ★
THE UNTHINKABLE

JIMMY KEPT HAVING TROUBLE BREATHING as he stared at the scene below them. He forced himself to take slow, deep breaths and try to think.

He had to do something.

Beside him, on their stomachs as well, Long, Zach, and Josh just stared.

Josh kept making long swallowing motions, like he was trying to hold his breakfast down. Jimmy had no doubt Josh was taking in every detail. He seemed to have a real skill for seeing things that others didn't, and then putting those details in his stories. This wasn't going to make good campfire reading, that was for sure.

Four men came out of the barn, laughing, leading two horses. Benson.

All Jimmy could do was stare at the man who had killed his parents. Something had to be done.

But any movement that they made down the hill at the men would just get them all killed as well.

Zach muttered something Jimmy couldn't hear and then pulled the rifle to his shoulder. He took aim, then lowered his rifle, stared at the scene below, then took aim again at the four men.

Jimmy reached over and put a hand on the gun.

When Zach glanced at him, Jimmy shook his head. It wasn't the time, and even though Zach was a good enough shot that he might get one or two of the killers, the other two would kill all the rest of them. That wasn't the way to do it. They had to come up with something else.

Zach looked like he was going to object, then finally nodded and lowered the rifle, his face white, his breath coming in gasps.

Jimmy forced himself to turn back and stare at the homestead and death below them, trying to see anything that was possible to do.

"Ideas?" he whispered to the others.

All three shook their heads.

Jimmy studied the trees behind the house. They would allow someone to get close, but then what?

Those men deserved to be hanged.

The thought echoed through his mind and Jimmy knew what they had to try to do. One at a time, they needed to pick off these men, separate them, bring them to justice. Even though he had promised his brother he wouldn't do anything until they were together, he couldn't wait any longer. Too many people were getting killed.

He turned to Josh. "The rope on my saddle, and Truitt's rope. Run and get both of them as quickly as you can. And bring all the horses and the other two up here right behind us. The sounds from the fire should cover the noise."

Long nodded in agreement.

Josh looked puzzled, then without a word scampered away.

Zach whispered to Jimmy. "What are you thinking?"

"We have to stop those men before more people get killed," Jimmy said, his voice barely in control. In all his life, he couldn't remember being this angry. "And the only way we're going to stop them is one at a time."

He quickly outlined his plan to Zach and Long.

Long and C.J. were the best two riders, so they would be the decoys. And C.J. had his special rock sling that might come in handy as well while he rode. It would be up to Jimmy and Truitt, with Zach standing guard with the rifle, to make the plan work.

Jimmy turned to Zach after he nodded agreement to the plan. "If you have to, can you really shoot a man?"

"I don't honestly know." Zach said, glancing down at the four men where they stood talking near the bodies of the family they had slaughtered. "But if I can't, I can at least give you cover."

Jimmy nodded. "Good enough. But it's going to be better to not fire a shot. The idea is to not let these men know what happened to one of them."

Zach nodded and went back to squeezing the stock of the rifle in nervousness.

Jimmy had no doubt they were in way over their heads with this plan. They were six basically green men taking on four deadly killers in the middle of the wilderness, with no chance of any help. More than likely, this was going to turn out badly.

But they had to try.

Jimmy just couldn't let more people be killed.

Zach and Jimmy went back over the hill to talk with the rest, leaving Long to stand guard.

"We have to move fast," Jimmy said after explaining the plan. "We will meet three miles off the trail in the trees just after dusk tonight, where we camped last night. Make sure none of the killers are following you."

Everyone nodded. Jimmy could tell they were all as afraid as he was, but all were willing to risk this.

Jimmy and Truitt each took a coil of rope. Jimmy put his over his shoulder so he could drop it quickly if he had to run. Then heading along the top of the hill, he and Truitt worked their way over and down into the trees behind the homestead.

Jimmy could see that Zach took up a position behind a rock on the hillside where he could see both Jimmy and Truitt. He was such a good shot that from there he could easily knock a man off his horse if he needed to.

And if he could.

Jimmy just hoped he wouldn't have to.

Silently, Jimmy moved from tree to tree through the grove along the stream, until he found a good tree beside an animal trail, then quickly went up it with one end of the rope. He hadn't climbed a tree in years, but it was a skill he hadn't forgotten.

About ten feet up, he settled into the crook of a branch, then quickly got his end of the rope around the tree trunk. Then he made sure he was braced and the rope was in place.

Truitt, on the other end of the rope in the tree on the other side of the trail, nodded that he was ready. They had the rope up high enough that anyone riding under it wouldn't notice it.

Jimmy gave Zach up on the hill the ready sign, and Zach turned and gave it to Josh.

Jimmy knew that if this didn't work, they might be trapped in these trees, and if that happened, he and Truitt would soon be dead.

Through the trees, Jimmy could see the killers getting ready to mount up.

Less than ten seconds later, with a blood-curdling war cry, Long and C.J. came riding around the edge of the ridge, their heads down, their horses going at full speed. Long had untied his hair and it flew out behind him like a cape.

And C.J. had wrapped himself in one of Long's Indian blankets and put some dirt on his face to make himself look more Indian, even with his glasses. To the four killers, it must have looked like Long and C.J. just appeared out of thin air not more than fifty paces away.

C.J. lifted up in his saddle only long enough to twirl his rock sling and hit one man solidly in the side with a rock.

The guy swore as he went to the ground, trying to get his gun out of his holster.

C.J. and Long rode past the killers on the other side of the burning homestead and headed into the trees behind the house where Jimmy and Truitt waited.

Benson had his gun out the quickest and fired, but the shot missed both C.J. and Long as they pushed into the trees and flashed right under Johnny and Truitt and the rope they held between them.

All four killers quickly mounted up and rode after Long and C.J., just as Jimmy knew they would. They didn't dare let any witness, even Indians, live to tell what they had done to that poor family.

C.J. and Long, once they got out of the trees down the stream, would split up and circle out over the hills to the north. Jimmy had no doubt that they could get away. They were both fantastic riders and had fast horses. Jimmy was far more worried about what he and Truitt were about to try. If they missed, one or both of them would be more than likely dead.

The man that C.J. had hit with his sling was a little slower mounting up than the other three and was trailing the other killers by a good twenty paces.

Benson and two of his men flashed past under Jimmy, the sounds of their swearing and horses' hoofs covering the sounds of the house burning.

Both Jimmy and Truitt timed the rope drop perfectly as the fourth man rode under them. The idea was to knock him off his horse, tie him up, and take him away before the other three got back.

The rope caught the man squarely across the upper chest. Perfect!

Jimmy had braced himself in the tree and had the rope wound around the trunk once, but the impact of a man being pulled off a horse at full run yanked Jimmy shoulder-first into the trunk. The rope burned in his hands as he fought to hold on.

Somehow, he did.

The killer swung up high in the air as the horse kept going, then dropped back.

The killer did a half turn in mid-air and landed on his head and shoulders on the trail.

There was a loud crack that echoed through the trees as the man hit.

Jimmy dropped the rope and climbed quickly out of the tree. His hands were shaking so badly, he could barely hang onto anything. Truitt's face looked white and his eyes were wide as they both scrambled to tie up the killer.

But by the time they had his hands tied, it was clear to Jimmy that they didn't need to do more. Jimmy dropped the rope and backed away like he was backing away from a snake.

Truitt did the same, muttering softly, "We weren't supposed to kill him."

"Get moving!" Zach shouted softly from up the hill.

"Let's go," Jimmy said, glancing up at Zach. "They might be back at any moment."

"What are we going to do?" Truitt asked, a sound of panic in his voice.

"Hide him, just like we planned," Jimmy said. He felt like he was about to be sick, but they couldn't stop now. They had to stay on the plan, even though the killer was dead.

Truitt nodded, took a deep breath, and seemed to come back into his eyes.

Jimmy quickly slipped the rope under the killer's arms, then at full run they dragged the man's body away from the trail and the burning building, deeper into the trees, using the rope around his chest to pull him like a sled. Near a rock ledge and the edge of the thick forest, they dropped the killer's body into a depression beside a tree, then frantically tossed some branches and dead grass over him.

Jimmy walked ten steps away and looked back. He couldn't see the body at all.

Truitt was still standing over the body staring at the killer.

Jimmy moved back over to his friend and put a hand on his shoulder. Truitt clearly had no problems taking things, or playing tricks on people, but he had never been near death.

"It was an accident," Jimmy said, trying to convince himself as much as Truitt. "Let's go."

Truitt nodded, took a deep breath, and turned. "I'll get his horse." He ran back toward the trees where the man's horse had stopped and was grazing.

With one last look at where they had hidden the killer's body, Jimmy headed back through the trees. He grabbed the two horses that Benson had planned on taking from the homestead. Benson wouldn't get them. Not this time.

Jimmy glanced around at the dead family. Right now, he couldn't do anything for them. They would come back after the other killers had gone.

As fast as he could, Jimmy climbed back up the hill, pulling the two horses behind him.

A few moments later, Zach and Truitt joined him with Josh and their horses. There were four of them and they now had seven horses.

"The fall killed him?" Josh asked, his face white, his hands twisting the notebook.

Jimmy nodded. "Broke his neck."

He was having a lot of problems with the fact that they had killed someone. But right now, he couldn't think about it. He had to get himself and his friends out of there and to safety.

"Let's get riding."

"Yeah, I'd like to be a long ways from here when Benson gets back," Zach said, putting the rifle in his saddle and mounting up quickly.

C.J. and Long were riding at full speed north. Jimmy, Truitt, Zach, and Josh, with the extra horses, would ride at the same speed south, then wait until almost dusk to circle around back to where they had camped last night.

With luck, they would all be there.

⋆ PART NINETEEN ⋆
BACK TOGETHER

THEY HAD ALL ARRIVED IN camp safely, with Long coming in last because he had wanted to make sure where Benson had gone. Long had the ability, because he was part Indian, to move silently and get amazingly close to things without ever being seen.

He told them that Benson and the other two killers had waited for their man for a while at the homestead, poked around a bit, then finally started down the trail at a good speed, clearly trying to put distance between them and the burning homestead.

Long said that there had been a lot of swearing and that Benson thought their "friend" had taken the horses and headed back up the trail, leaving them.

Or maybe the Indians had gotten him.

Good news to Jimmy. They did not suspect they were behind them.

Jimmy still posted three guards that night, and they hadn't built a fire.

They didn't dare let Benson find them, not after what Benson had done to that family.

Jimmy hadn't slept much at all, and the only time he managed to fall asleep, he had a nightmare of the dead killer and the family standing and politely applauding. It was a horrid nightmare that woke him up sweating and made him take over guard duty an hour sooner than he was supposed to.

He couldn't believe he had killed a man. Even as an accident, did that make him as bad as Benson? He tried to push that thought away, but it kept coming back over and over all night long.

The next morning, Long scouted ahead and finally found Benson and his two remaining men moving west down the California Trail. They seemed to be pacing behind a small wagon company.

An hour later, they headed back and arrived back at the homestead and slowly dismounted. The building was still smoldering, sending a thin line of smoke into the clear blue sky.

"We need to bury these folks," Zach said, picking up the shovel the boy had been carrying when he was shot in the back.

Jimmy nodded and looked around. The ridge where he and the others had watched yesterday would be perfect. "Up there, where they can stand watch for all time over their homestead."

Silently, all six boys went looking for what it was going to take to dig three graves, get the bodies up the hill, and get this done.

Two long hours later, they were all hot and sweating, but they had the family in the ground with crosses over each grave. It reminded Jimmy far too much of when he and his brother had buried his parents.

Benson had to be stopped.

"I wish we knew their names," C.J. said.

"The Goose Creek family," Josh said. "As long as we remember them, they will live on."

"No way to forget this," Truitt said. "I'm going to be having nightmares for months."

"Yeah, me too," both Jimmy and Zach said at the same time.

"Should we do anything about him?" Zach asked, pointing to the trees where the body of the killer was.

"Let the animals have him," Long said, disgusted.

"He was a human," C.J. said, taking his glasses off his face and wiping sweat from his forehead. "He deserves something."

"He killed this family," Zach said, pointing up the hill at the graves they had just dug. "He doesn't deserve anything."

"We'll put some rocks on him," Jimmy said, staring up into the trees. He was having enough trouble with the death of the killer. He couldn't have the thought of animals getting the man in his mind.

"I'll help you," Truitt said.

All six boys helped, and in fifteen minutes they had the man under a cairn of rocks. They didn't mark the grave.

As they came out of the trees toward the barn, a stage came into sight from the west, pulled by a team of six horses.

During the trip west, they had passed a number of large wagons and stages going east. All of the stages had been Butterfield Stages, carrying mostly letters and a few passengers who didn't mind getting tossed around inside a stagecoach for a few thousand miles.

The stage pulled up in a wide area just off the trail and the boys went down to meet it.

"What happened?" the driver asked, his hand on his gun. His co-driver had his rifle up and ready.

Jimmy understood their fear. The house had been burned down, and these two men had no idea that Jimmy and his friends hadn't done it.

Jimmy told them what they had found, and then who had done it. None of them said a word about what they had done to Benson's man yesterday.

"We buried the family up on the hill," Jimmy said.

"There are three men tucked in a few miles behind a wagon company about a half day up the trail," the driver said, clearly relaxing, taking his hand off his gun. "Not much we can do."

"Out here, there's not much anyone can do," Zach said.

"Ain't that the truth," the driver said.

Jimmy described Benson and the driver nodded. "That was the man. It's too bad, too. The Bennetts were good people. Thanks for burying them. You boys stay away from those three."

"We will," Jimmy said to the driver, even though he knew they wouldn't.

Josh and C.J. got the Bennetts' full names from the driver. Josh wrote them down carefully, then the two of them went back up the hill to put the names on the crosses.

Jimmy asked the driver if he could send a letter along to someone in Independence and the driver said sure. Jimmy wrote a quick note to his brother Luke, care of Doc Davis, and gave it to the driver. He offered to pay for the letter's delivery, but the driver just tucked it in his pocket. "You've paid for the letter by burying our friends."

The stage left and they all paid their last respects to the family on the hill. Then, as they were back near the barn silently getting ready to mount back up, Long held up his hand. "Do you hear that?"

Jimmy strained to hear something besides the wind in the trees and the distant sound of some fast water in the creek. Nothing, but

Jimmy had come to accept that Long could hear and see things that none of the rest of them could. It was an amazing special ability.

Long handed his horse lead to Zach and went back toward the smoldering house, quickly and silently.

Finally, Jimmy heard what Long had heard.

A faint whimper.

Something was alive back there.

But how could that be possible?

Long and Jimmy went to the right of the cabin, Zach with his gun out went to the left. C.J. had his rock sling out and was right behind Jimmy.

On the other side of the burnt-out building, they all stopped.

Jimmy held his breath, listening to the sound of the stream and the faint wind in the leaves of the trees.

Then the sound came again.

A whimper.

Long turned and moved around behind a few trees. There, he pulled open what looked like a sod-covered door on a root cellar that none of them had noticed tucked behind a tree next to the hill.

Inside, sitting on the stairs, was a young boy, about seven years of age.

He blinked at the bright light, then covered his head and started crying.

It took an hour or so for the boys to get the child calmed down and some water and food in him. He said between sobs that his name was Arthur.

Jimmy knew they certainly couldn't take Arthur with them, but they also couldn't just leave him either.

Jimmy pulled Zach aside. "We need to get the kid back to Fort Hall."

"That's a hundred miles back," Zach said. "I can do it."

"Or find someone in a wagon company who will take him," Jimmy said. He didn't much like the idea of Zach not being at his side. There had to be a better choice.

"A wagon train is unlikely," Zach said. "Fort Hall with the military is his best bet. Unless we can catch up to that Butterfield Stage." He didn't sound hopeful, and Jimmy doubted they could. Those stages moved fast, and kept going, changing horses all the time.

Jimmy stood thinking for a moment, staring at the three crosses on the hill above them. He knew that Zach was right, and he was the best person to do the ride because he was the most responsible of all of them.

"Take along the two horses that we rescued," Jimmy said. "They belong to the kid now anyhow. They might help him get a home. And give him the killer's saddle and gear. Truitt can go with you."

Zach nodded.

"If you don't catch us by Virginia City," Jimmy said, "we'll wait for you there." Virginia City was on the other side of Nevada from where they were, up against the Sierras and the final mountain passes over into California. At a good speed, they were still three weeks away from there, but with Benson moving slowly ahead of them, Jimmy doubted they would be moving very fast at all.

Zach nodded. "If we ride solid, it won't take anywhere near that long. We should be back with you by the time you are down on the Humboldt. Maybe ten days."

"That's what I was figuring," Jimmy said.

Twenty minutes later, Zach and Truitt headed back east with the young boy saddled up on one of his horses.

The other four continued west, using the killer's horse as a packhorse. They still had three killers to track and try to stop.

⋆ PART TWENTY ⋆
ON A KILLER'S TRAIL

THE NEXT DAY, JIMMY, LONG, Josh, and C.J. caught up with Benson and his men again just after the trail crested over a slight range of hills and dropped down onto Dead Horse Creek.

The hills were covered in sparse dry grass and sagebrush. Only the areas along the creek were green. This area felt a lot more like a desert to Jimmy than anything they had come through, giving them almost no protection from the hot sun. The rock bluffs along the stream were brown, and sometimes towered a good hundred feet into the air above the shallow creek.

The coach driver had been right, Benson and his three men were following a few miles behind a small wagon company with only eight wagons. Only having eight wagons was just asking for problems. Usually the companies were far larger when they left Independence.

More than likely, this was just part of a larger company that had slowly split apart over the long months of travel.

Long scouted ahead, watching Benson and his men, as the rest of them stayed back and out of sight. Jimmy was convinced that Benson planned on robbing the train at some point. The questions were when and where.

And more importantly, how could Jimmy and the rest of them do something to stop it? This time, he didn't want to kill any of them. The accidental killing of one of Benson's gang bothered Jimmy a lot. He wasn't about to let his friends become like Benson and his gang.

That evening, the train made camp up against a tall rock bluff, with the wagons in a loose circle to protect the middle of the camp. Benson and his men camped back a few miles near a bend in the stream in some small trees.

Jimmy had the boys get off the trail and make camp on top of the bluffs above the wagons and far enough away from the company that their fire wouldn't be seen.

"So, how are we going to stop Benson from robbing that wagon train?" Jimmy asked after they had a fire going. The sun was still an hour from setting and Jimmy figured they had just about that much time to do something.

Josh held up some weeds. "This might do it," he said.

C.J. pushed his glasses down his nose and stared at the weeds in Josh's hands. "You want to poison them? That's called locoweed and it drives cattle crazy."

Jimmy had never seen anything like it, and he was surprised that both Josh and C.J. knew what it was. It had been along the trail for miles.

"My people use it in special ceremonies," Long said. "It makes you see things that cannot be seen. It will not kill taken in small amounts."

Jimmy laughed, then stared at Long. "Think you can get some of that into Benson's and his men's food if we gave you a diversion? That ought to keep them from robbing anyone tonight."

Long nodded. "They are cooking beans and coffee they took from the homestead."

"What do you need for a diversion?"

Long moved over toward the rocks without saying a word, then moving faster than Jimmy could see, he grabbed into a hole and picked up something. When he turned around, Jimmy could see it was a very angry, very large rattlesnake. The rattle on the end of its tail was making an intense noise. "Their horses will not like this," Long said, holding up the huge snake he held behind the head.

"I don't like it," C.J. said, backing away.

Long held the snake with one hand while he watched Josh chop up some of the weeds into tiny bits, then smash them between two rocks until he had a fine powder. Long held out his empty hand and Josh brushed the powder into his hand.

"Follow me," Long said. "I will show you where you can watch their camp."

A few minutes later, Jimmy, C.J., and Josh were hiding behind rocks as Long worked his way down toward the killer's camp. The three were sitting around the fire, clearly getting ready to eat. Their three horses were tied up in the trees about thirty paces from their fire.

Long got close, tossed the snake into the middle of the horses, then ducked down behind a large rock near the three men. Jimmy would have been scared to death getting that close to those three killers like that, but clearly Long had very little fear of them.

Their horses went crazy, rearing back against their ties, trying to get away from the angry rattlesnake.

All three killers reacted as one, jumping up and running for the horses.

Almost like a ghost, Long appeared near their food and drink and put powder in both, then vanished back behind a rock.

It was everything Jimmy and Josh and C.J. could do to not laugh. They ducked down to make sure they weren't seen, and after a few minutes, Long joined them.

The four boys watched the killers eat. At first, nothing seemed to be happening. They cleaned up their camp, put out their fire, and got ready to ride out as it started to get dark. Clearly, they were still planning on robbing the wagon company.

Then Jimmy noticed that one of the killers tried to get on his horse and missed, falling into the dirt. The other two laughed and pointed and laughed.

"The plan seems to be working," Josh said.

"But not enough," Jimmy said as the three rode laughing toward the wagon company.

⋆ PART TWENTY-ONE ⋆
ONE MORE PLAN

"CAN WE GET TO A PLACE above the wagons without being seen?" Jimmy asked as the three killers rode off. He couldn't let Benson and his men kill more innocent people. He just couldn't.

"What are you thinking?" Josh asked, looking worried.

"No plans yet," Jimmy said. "But I'm open for all kinds of ideas. We can't let those monsters kill an entire company of people"

"I agree," C.J. said, patting his sling. "I just wish Zach had left the rifle."

Jimmy felt his stomach clamp at that. They were unarmed against three armed killers.

"This way," Long said, vanishing back into the darkness.

It took them a good thirty minutes on foot to get to the bluff over the wagons. By that point, there had been shots and women screaming.

The sound had made Jimmy' blood go cold and his heart race. This couldn't be happening again.

Not again.

A half-dozen cook fires lit up the area under them, making it seem like a bright day among the wagons. Benson had killed what must have been the train's leader, and two of the killers were holding two women with guns to their heads. The rest of the families were standing helpless, just watching. The killers were weaving back and forth like they were drunk, and laughing at anything.

There had to be twenty men and women in that train, plus another ten children.

Jimmy knew that most of them were going to die unless they did something, and did it fast.

Jimmy signaled that they should move back from the edge, then turned to C.J. and Josh, the two smartest of them all. "Any ideas?"

"We have surprise on our side," Josh said. "They don't know we're here."

"And we have the darkness to help us," C.J. said. "We can spook them into running since they have so much Loco weed in them."

"I can do a very frightening Bannock war cry," Long said. "If I ride through the shadows near their horse making the cry, they might think they are surrounded by Bannock."

Jimmy nodded. "Especially if we are pelting them with rocks at the same time."

C.J. laughed and whipped out his homemade sling. "They won't even know what hit them."

Three boys with rocks against three men with guns.

Jimmy had no doubt they were going to have to be very lucky to get away with this attack.

Very lucky if they lived, actually.

He couldn't believe that for the second time in three days he was going to attack Benson and his men. It was crazy.

"Long, when we hear you coming, we'll start throwing," Jimmy said.

"Five minutes," Long said, nodding and then vanishing silently into the darkness back toward their camp and their horses.

Jimmy went on. "C.J., you take the younger killer, Josh, you take the other one. "I'll take Benson. Make sure you are in a sheltered place with a lot of rocks to throw when they start shooting. And if your man leaves the light, we all run."

Long and C.J. nodded.

"This is going to be fun," C.J. said, laughing.

Josh just shook his head.

Jimmy would have never called this fun. Crazy, yes, deadly, yes, but never fun.

They all spread out along the top of the cliff, picking up fist-sized rocks as they went.

Jimmy found at least a dozen and put himself behind a large rock that allowed him shelter, but if he leaned out and forward, he could clearly see the camp below.

His heart was beating so hard, he was sure Benson could hear it.

"Okay," he said softly to himself. "Make each throw deadly."

At that moment, an echoing Bannock war cry filled the air, sending shivers down Jimmy's back. It seemed to hang in the night air, echoing off the rocks like there was more than one call.

Long was right, that was something that would frighten enemies and friends alike.

Long came flashing into the light, past the fire, and back into the darkness. All three killers spun around, guns aimed into the darkness, but they had so much locoweed in them, they barely stood up.

Jimmy took a deep breath, stood and threw the rock at Benson as hard as he could.

Benson was standing in the middle of the camp, near a fire, staring after the ghost-like image of Long.

The rock fell a few feet short, bounced once and slammed into Benson's shin.

Benson snapped forward and grabbed his leg, swearing and clearly in pain.

In all his life, Jimmy had never felt such a thrill as that moment. Maybe C.J. was right.

Maybe this would be fun.

An echoing Bannock war cry again filled the air, sending more shivers down Jimmy's back. The people in the wagon company dove for cover under the wagons as the three killers stood their ground under the rocks from above.

All three killers started firing up at the cliff face, but their aim was random and far off target.

Long flashed past the camp again, coming in closer behind the men, screaming out his war cry.

Jimmy missed with his second rock, but his third throw hit Benson squarely in the chest and knocked him to his back in the dirt.

Before he could get up, Jimmy hit him with another rock, this time in the back, sending him back to the ground.

The gunfire had stopped.

The two killers came running toward Benson, heading past him at a mad dash for their horses. They were clearly as scared as a grown man could get.

Long's war cry again filled the night air.

Jimmy was throwing as hard and as fast as he could, letting his anger at Benson power his arm.

A rock from C.J.'s sling caught the youngest of Benson's men in the arm, clearly breaking it. The other man was bleeding from a head wound and limping from the attack that Josh had waged on him.

Jimmy kept throwing, fast and hard, not letting the man who had killed his parents have a moment's rest.

To the men below, it must have seemed as if the dark night sky had opened up and just dumped rocks at them.

Long screamed out the Bannock war cry again.

It made Jimmy shiver, and even Benson's horses reared up at the sound.

Jimmy's aim was getting better. He hit Benson squarely in the shoulder as he climbed to his feet, spinning the man around and forcing him to drop his gun.

Benson scrambled on all fours for his gun as Jimmy hit him in the back with another rock, sending him to his stomach.

Finally, Benson scrambled up, turned and limped behind his men for his horse.

Jimmy managed to hit him one more time in the back of his leg before Benson got mounted and rode at full speed west, out of the camp, following his two men down the California Trail.

There was silence in the wagon camp.

Jimmy knew that Long would follow the killers for a distance, terrorizing them, making sure they didn't turn back on the wagon company.

Below them, the stunned people of the wagon company scrambled for their weapons and got ready to defend themselves as well. It was going to take a little explaining as to why they wouldn't have to.

"Well," C.J. said from somewhere in the darkness. "Shall we go down and say hello?"

"I don't see why not," Jimmy said, laughing, feeling better than he had felt in a long, long time. They had beat Benson once more.

Now Jimmy knew they could somehow do it again.

And again.

Until the killer was finally brought to justice.

Jimmy looked down at the stunned people staring upward into the darkness, waiting for more rocks to come flying, then laughed again. "It seems they might owe us a dinner."

⋆ PART TWENTY-TWO ⋆
HEADED TOWARD DANGER

MORE THAN THREE WEEKS HAD passed since Zach and Truitt had rejoined them from taking the young boy back. It had been the longest and hottest three weeks Jimmy could ever remember. They had followed slowly, very slowly, behind the wagon train that Benson and his men were shadowing.

Long reported that one of Benson's men, the one with the broken arm, seemed to be getting weaker and weaker, which got a cheer from everyone. It had been C.J., with his special sling, that had hit the man in the arm with a rock.

They were all proud of the fact that they had rescued an entire wagon company from Benson and his killers. To Jimmy, after not being in time to save the family at the homestead, saving the fine people of that wagon company had felt wonderful.

The people of the company had been very appreciative as well, wanting the boys to ride along with them the rest of the way to California.

Even though there were some pretty girls Jimmy's age with the company, all of them had decided to move on, to stay close behind Benson and his men.

The trail across most of Northern Nevada wound in and out of the desert scrub and rocks beside the ever-smaller flow of the Humboldt River. They had had to cross the river seven times, but the flow was so small, the crossings hadn't ever been a problem.

As C.J. and Josh had told them, ahead was the Humboldt Sink, where what was left of the river just vanished into desert.

And beyond that, the hardest leg of the trip, the Forty Mile Desert.

Every day along the Humboldt, the temperatures were unbearable in the afternoon, so they had adopted a travel method of getting up before dawn and moving in the early light, then by noon finding a shelter of either brush or rocks and resting during the hot hours.

Long kept great care of their horses, making sure they were fed and watered the right amounts, but even with the good care and decent grass, the heat was clearly taking a toll on them. A week earlier, Long had shifted the horse C.J. was riding to a packhorse because it couldn't carry C.J.'s weight and his gear anymore.

Along the river, Jimmy was stunned at how many broken-down wagons littered the trail. At each wagon without people, Jimmy had them search for water bags and smaller supplies that might come in handy. They had found a few water bags and a canteen.

With what Jimmy understood they were facing, trying to carry extra water might just be what saved their lives.

Years and years of dead stock bones, bleached white, littered the sides of the trail as well. There weren't that many wagon companies ahead of them yet this summer, since they were traveling by horse, but even so, there were already dozens of fresh dead animals beside the trail, most of them torn apart by packs of wild dogs Josh said were called coyotes.

Jimmy couldn't imagine what it was going to be like when all the wagons behind them got here, in the heat of August. The entire trail would smell like death almost every step of the way.

They had had to pass at least four solo wagons with families. They had broken down and been left by their companies who had had no choice but to move on.

They had stopped to see if they could help at each family, but there was really nothing they could do. The families all seemed to have water and food. Jimmy figured that with luck, the families would join up with another company coming along, either with their wagon fixed or walking the rest of the way. Otherwise, if at some point they didn't move forward, those families, children and all, would just die in the extreme heat of the desert.

As each day went by, and the farther they got down the Humboldt, the more graves there were, all with names roughly scratched into wooden crosses.

Josh started to write down all the names and locations, but after a week on the Humboldt, there were so many, he gave up the task as too depressing.

Two days away from the Humboldt Sink, Josh read them all a passage from his favorite writer, Mark Twain, who had been out west a few years earlier and had written about the Forty Mile Desert.

Twain said, "It would hardly be an exaggeration to say that we could have walked the forty miles and set our feet on a bone at every step."

"Okay, no more of that," Truitt said, shaking his head. "We still have to cross that thing."

With the intense heat, all the bones and graves along the Humboldt, and forty miles of sand ahead of them, Jimmy could imagine Twain being very, very right about what they were facing.

Jimmy sure wasn't looking forward to that leg on this adventure.

★ PART TWENTY-THREE ★
KNOWING WHAT'S AHEAD

THE WAGON COMPANY THAT BENSON was following camped for three days on the edge of the Sink, so they were forced to camp back down the trail a half-day's ride to make sure they weren't seen.

Just sitting, not moving, bothered Jimmy more than anything. But Long said it was a good thing, since they were resting the horses, and gaining all their strength before crossing the Forty Mile Desert.

With the wagon company camped like that, Long was able to get much closer. It seemed, from what Long overheard, that some of the men of the company had died during a river crossing early in the trip, and now there were only five men and three older boys in the seven wagons, with a dozen young children and ten women.

Long said Benson and his men were pretending they were going to help the company across the desert.

"Not likely," Jimmy had said. "It's only a matter of time before those people meet a very sad end."

"Unless we can do something to stop Benson," Josh said.

"I'm open to any ideas," Jimmy said.

They talked about it for most of the evening and all of the next day, but no one could come up with anything that would allow them to stop Benson and not get killed.

The wagon company was camped right out in the open, above the water, with no place around the wagon camp to surprise Benson with any kind of attack. And at night, the company had two men standing guard at all times. Usually one of them was one of Benson's men, or Benson himself.

Finally, they all agreed to try to warn one of the men of the wagon company when he got away from the train. It was the best plan they could think of.

Jimmy and Long, just before dawn on the second morning, met one of the younger men from the train while he was out trying to gather wood for a fire. He wasn't much older than they were, and looked very tired and worn out. His clothes were tattered and he looked underfed. Fighting wagons along this trail could do that to a man.

After they had told him about Benson and his two men, the guy had only nodded. "Thanks for the warning, but we don't trust them either. We won't let them get the drop on us." He patted the six-shooter he had tucked into his belt.

"If you need our help, we're camped back down the trail," Jimmy said.

The guy nodded. "We won't. Thanks again, though."

"Just don't tell Benson we're behind you," Jimmy said.

"Oh, trust me," the man had said with a shake of his head, "I don't even talk to those men."

With that, he walked back toward the wagon company carrying an armload of sticks.

Jimmy had no doubt that the warning wouldn't help. If Benson followed his true nature, that man would be dead very shortly.

But there was nothing he or the rest of them could do, so they went back to waiting.

Jimmy wasn't so sure how rested they were getting in the extreme heat. The air just seemed to take any energy he had out of his body, and it wasn't until long after the sun went down and the air cooled that he even started to feel like moving at all.

One night, around the campfire, Josh and C.J. filled them all in on what was coming for them in the desert.

"Most companies start across the desert at night," Josh said, "leaving the camp near the Sink to cross the fifteen miles that it takes to even reach the drop down into the Forty Mile Desert."

"It's well over fifty miles from the last water to the Truckee River," C.J. said.

Together, they all worked out a plan.

Jimmy hadn't liked the sound of anything that was coming.

Fifty-five miles in sand, without water.

They were going to have to be very, very ready for the crossing.

Finally, coming back just after dawn on the third morning, Long reported that the wagon company, with Benson and his men helping them, had started to make the crossing. "They left one wagon behind," Long said, "but no people."

"We go tonight," Jimmy said. "Let's move up to their old camp and get ready. That will give them a full day's head start. We don't want to catch them somewhere out there in the middle of that sand."

"Good idea," Truitt said. "They won't be stopping, that's for sure."

"Neither will we," C.J. said. "Stopping in that desert is the quickest way to die."

"Sounds like a good time," Zach said, shaking his head.

"Before we leave," Jimmy said, "we need to make sure every water bag is full, every canteen."

"I'll have the stock well watered," Long said. "But we're going to need every drop we don't drink for the horses to get them across as well. And we'll have to pack extra grass."

When they reached the campsite beside the Sink, they could clearly see the six wagons kicking up dust far out on a vast open expanse of light brown sand.

They found shelter under some trees and settled in.

For Jimmy, the heat of the day seemed to drag on and on.

California was just over those mountains in the distance. Somewhere, between here and Sacramento, he needed to get his father's gold mine deed back from Benson.

He just didn't know how yet.

All of them tried to stay in the shade as long as the sun was out, and from where Jimmy was sitting, by mid-afternoon, he could no longer see the dust trail from the wagons.

Tomorrow, instead of resting in the shade, they would be moving in the heat. Once you started across the desert, there was no stopping.

A lot of things had happened on the trip west, but right now, what faced them frightened him more than anything had frightened him before.

But they had no choice.

If they stopped, they died.

★ PART TWENTY-FOUR ★
STARTING ACROSS HELL

AS AN ALMOST FULL MOON came up over the hot desert, they broke camp. Every canteen, every water bag was brimming full. Then, with each of them taking one last, long drink from the fresh water near the camp, they started off.

"Stay between the wagon wheel ruts," Long said, taking the lead as he usually did. "Safer in the dark."

Jimmy was last in line and was leading one packhorse.

Zach led another packhorse behind Long.

Then it was C.J., Josh, and Truitt in that order.

They kept close to each other and after a while Jimmy noticed that his eyes had adjusted and he could see pretty well in just the light from the moon.

They moved steadily.

As the night got cooler, Long had them pick up the pace. They needed to cover as much ground as possible when it was cool and dark.

They made the fifteen miles to the edge of the desert without any problems. The moon was directly over their heads as they reached the edge of the Forty Mile Desert.

They stopped for a few minutes rest on the top of the ridge before dropping down the steep incline to the desert floor.

At first, Jimmy didn't understand what he was seeing. The trail was framed all the way down the slope to the level desert floor with piles and piles of white.

Then it suddenly dawned on him what he was actually looking at. Bones.

Thousands of animals' bones lined both sides of the trail down the hill like a horrid decoration of a nightmarish garden path.

"Ready?" he asked everyone, tearing his gaze away from the bones.

"Not really," C.J. said.

"We've come this far," Truitt said, "we can't let forty miles of sand stop us."

"One at a time down this slope," Long said, mounting up and starting down between the rows of white animal bones gleaming in the moonlight.

Long made it to the bottom fine, and so did Zach with his packhorse.

Truitt went next, then Josh, both signaling they were at the bottom with a whistle.

Jimmy sat on his horse at the top, watching C.J.

Everything seemed to be going fine until suddenly, about halfway down, C.J.'s horse stumbled and went down, dumping C.J. into the deep sand.

C.J. rolled down the hill and came up spitting sand.

Long and Zach, on foot, quickly climbed back up to him while Jimmy led his horses down slowly from the top.

C.J. was fine, but his horse had broken a leg.

They got the supplies and water off the horse and distributed to the other horses. Then C.J., with Long's help, saddled their best packhorse with his gear.

The horse with the broken leg had been one Jimmy's father had bought in St. Louis. For some reason, it suddenly felt as if he was going to lose another member of his family.

He felt sick.

As Jimmy watched, and Long turned his back, Zach did the hardest job he had ever had to do.

He led the horse over to where there was a large pile of white bones that were piled almost waist high.

Then, with one clean shot from the rifle, he put the suffering horse down.

Just like with much of what they had had to do on this trip, there just wasn't a choice.

It was life, or it was death.

And to Jimmy, here in the Wild West, there didn't seem to be much between the two.

★ PART TWENTY-FIVE ★
INTO THE DESERT

FOR THE NEXT TWO HOURS, as the sun started to color the sky in reds and browns, they rode in silence, moving at a fast pace across the flat sand while it was still cool. Then, just before the sun came up, Jimmy had them stop and rest and water the horses.

"From here," Long said, "we go slowly."

Long and Truitt and C.J. took care of the horses while Jimmy and Zach and Josh checked to make sure all the water was secured, protected from direct sun, and not leaking. With the day they had ahead of them, they were going to need every drop.

C.J. figured they had gone at least twenty-five of the over fifty-five miles to the Truckee River.

The easy half was all Jimmy could think.

The next thirty miles, the sun would bake them as dry as an overcooked biscuit, as Truitt would say.

As the sun crested the distant ridge, they started out again, the horses wading slowly in the soft sand.

The farther they got into the desert, the more bones and remains of wagons they found. Some of the remains had been there for years, others were fairly new. Jimmy had no doubt that by the time the summer was finished, and all the wagon companies behind them had crossed this, there would be many, many more broken dreams littering this nightmarish place.

It seemed that Mark Twain's description of this desert was very accurate.

At one point, C.J. pointed out a pile of bones ten feet off to one side of the trail. It took Jimmy a moment to realize what he was looking at in the hot sun.

Human bones.

Maybe three people, their bones piled like firewood, their skulls gaping at the sand around them.

And from that point on, they saw more and more human bones. Out here, the people who were still alive didn't dare stop and bury anyone. They just left them beside the trail and pushed on.

They had no choice.

They now stopped every hour to rest and feed and water the horses. Jimmy drank what he thought he should to make the water last, but it never felt like enough.

With the sun moving higher in the sky, the temperatures climbed, making him feel like he was standing far too close to a raging fire.

The glare off the sand was blinding, and waves of heat just radiated up like the sand itself was on fire.

To Jimmy, the short stops seemed almost worse than moving forward, but he knew they had to do them, to pace this journey.

At one point, about an hour after dawn, they came across a bubbling hot springs, the water so hot that steam filled the air around it even in the dry heat. There was no reason for even trying to cool and drink the water, since it smelled like sulfur.

Josh said that someone reported that there used to be a sign here that said, "If you can't go forward, you won't survive going back."

"The sign is a myth," C.J. said. "But more than likely the meaning is very true."

Truitt said something about now knowing where the devil Lved as they went past the bubbling, hot sulfur water.

★ PART TWENTY-SIX ★
ONE DOWN

JIMMY WATCHED TRUITT SWAY FOR a moment side-to-side in his saddle like he was on a boat in high waves, then tumble off his horse and land with a thud in the hot, desert sand.

"Truitt's down!" Jimmy shouted to the others ahead of him, panic filling his gut like a bad meal. He jumped off his horse and scrambled in the deep sand to where his friend lay. He felt like he was running through deep water, the sand was so soft. It fought him every step.

He knelt beside Truitt, the hot sand burning through his pants. Carefully, he turned his friend over and brushed the sand away from his mouth and eyes, moving Truitt's brown hair off his forehead at the same time. Truitt's skin was red and he was breathing shallowly.

"Truitt? Can you hear me?"

Truitt moaned, but didn't open his eyes.

They couldn't lose Truitt. Not now. Not here.

Long ran up with the rest and knelt in the sand. He quickly unscrewed a canteen and poured a little water on Truitt's forehead. The sand and dirt turned to a thin mud and dried in streamers down his cheeks almost instantly in the intense heat.

Long glanced over at Jimmy. "Open his mouth."

Jimmy pried open Truitt's mouth with his fingers and Long poured the water in slowly. Truitt choked for a moment, coughed, then drank.

After a moment which seemed like an eternity, it was as if Long had given him a magic medicine. Truitt blinked, opened his eyes, looked at the five men hovering over him, and then asked in a soft whisper, "What happened?"

Long gave him another drink of water, then stood. "Heat."

He pulled out a piece of buffalo jerky from his belt pouch and handed it to Truitt. "Chew on this and drink."

Truitt made a face, but did as Long said. None of them liked how salty Long's jerky was, but they all trusted Long when it came to anything having to do with survival out in the west. And right now, here in the middle of the Forty Mile Desert, the most dangerous stretch of the California Trail, they really needed his special skills to stay alive.

"Everyone, water and jerky," Long said, taking a drink himself and then taking out a piece of buffalo jerky. Long had spent nights smoking the jerky back after leaving Fort Hall, and Truitt had complained that Long had used a lot of their salt provisions for the process.

All Long had said was, "We will need it salty." He hadn't explained, and no one had asked. It was now, in the heat, that for some reason, Long wanted them all eating the salty jerky.

After they got out of this, if they got out of this, Jimmy would ask him why.

Jimmy moved away from Truitt and stood beside the horses, letting his wide-brimmed hat protect his face from the glaring sun. He then did as the others, working on the jerky and washing it down with water. They had carried into the Forty Mile Desert as much water as they could, but they were going through it alarmingly fast.

Long and Zach gave water to the horses. Joshua and C.J. sat in the shade their horses offered, drinking and chewing on the buffalo jerky.

Truitt had managed to move over beside C.J. in the slight shade of one horse and was looking better by the minute.

Jimmy turned and looked back the way they had come. The drifting sand made it impossible to see anything but the distant low hills. In the other direction, ahead, through the haze of the hot summer day, were the mountains of the Sierras. They looked to be both invitingly close, and impossibly distant.

And somewhere, just ahead of them, Jake Benson and his two remaining men were moving with a wagon company. Benson had killed Jimmy's parents, shot his brother, and then had killed another family back on Goose Creek, on the east side of Nevada.

At night, Jimmy was still haunted by the man they had accidentally killed at that homestead, but during the day, Jimmy just didn't let himself think about it. That man had been one of the men who had killed Jimmy's parents, and the family on the homestead, and who knew how many others. Yet Jimmy still hated the fact that the man had died. That wasn't what they had planned.

And the accident had given him many, many nightmares over the past weeks. He had no doubt, it was going to haunt him for a lot longer.

He pushed the thought away. Right now, Benson and his men were ahead of them, in the desert, pretending to help a small company of wagons. More than likely, Benson was going to rob and kill the fine people in the wagons somewhere in the middle of this horrible desert, but there was nothing Jimmy or any of the others could do about it. They had even tried to warn the people, but had been ignored.

"Keep eating and drinking," Long said. "We'll rest the horses for another ten minutes."

Jimmy nodded. Even though Jimmy was mostly in charge of the group, when it came to the horses, Long was in charge. He knew how to keep them alive and moving west, and that was all that mattered.

Jimmy looked at the distant mountains and wondered if he would ever see them. They had a long way left to go to get across this desert, and their water supply was going down fast. Without water, what happened to Truitt would happen to them all in the intense heat.

Very quickly.

★ PART TWENTY-SEVEN ★
MORE TROUBLE AHEAD

AFTER THEY RESTED AND HAD eaten the jerky and drank enough water, Long said to Jimmy. "We need to walk from here. The horses can't carry us much farther in this deep sand and in this heat."

Jimmy agreed.

Long had warned them all this would happen. It was part of their plan So, on foot, they started out again, leading their horses.

Each step felt to Jimmy like he was sinking in quicksand, as the desert wanted to not let his boot go.

He tried to stay in the wagon tracks, but often missed and stumbled, using the reins of his horse to keep himself from falling face down.

Every step drained more and more energy.

Every mile was a torture.

It wasn't even the hottest time of the day yet, yet the air felt like he was inside a hot oven.

An hour later, as they crested a slight rise in the desert floor about three hours after dawn, they could see the seven wagons that Benson had been "helping" across the desert.

They were stopped dead in the trail and there were no signs of people or the oxen and horses that had been pulling them.

Jimmy wanted to stop short, let Long scout ahead and see what was happening, but both C.J. and Josh said, "We can't stop. We have to go past them."

Jimmy glanced at Long, who clearly agreed with C.J. and Josh.

If they stopped, they died.

If Benson was still with those wagons, they were going to have to take the chance and walk right past him.

Jimmy didn't like that idea at all.

In fact, that idea scared him almost as much as this desert did.

"We ride the next mile until we're past those wagons," Jimmy said.

Long agreed and had everyone give their horse a drink.

Back in the saddle, even moving slowly, it didn't seem to take them long to cross the next mile of desert.

Jimmy now wasn't focused on the sun, but on what was ahead. He hardly took his eye off those wagons.

There was no sign at all of life.

Nothing was moving, not even the canvas tops of the wagons, since there was no wind at all in this forsaken place.

The closer they got, the more likely it was looking that Benson and his men had robbed the poor wagon company, killed everyone and left.

Twice so far, in the thick sand, the trail had gone around what had been a stopped wagon company some years before. Those wagons had been weather-beaten and the white bones of stock and people littered everywhere. Now this wagon company had stopped right in the middle of the trail as well, and it didn't look as if those wagons were ever going another foot forward.

There were no oxen or horses left with the wagons to pull them.

As they got close enough to see details, it became clear that what they were seeing was a massacre.

Benson and his men had struck again.

All the men and boys were scattered around the wagons, some laying face down in the sand, others face up. They were clearly all dead. A couple of them had guns in their hands, including the man Jimmy and Long had talked to.

It seemed he had been wrong. He had let Benson get the drop on him.

Jimmy had no idea why they hadn't heard the shooting. Maybe sound didn't carry well over the sand.

"No women," Zach said as they got closer.

Jimmy was surprised he hadn't noticed that. There weren't any women's or children's bodies in sight at all. Maybe Benson and his men had taken them.

Then Long pointed to one man's body and Jimmy recognized him as one of Benson's men. It was the one with the broken arm. It looked like he had just passed out and died right where he lay. Or maybe one of the wagon men had shot him.

Long led them in a wide circle around the wagons, starting what would become the new trail through the sand.

It wasn't until they passed the last wagon in line that Truitt shouted, "The women!"

At first, Jimmy didn't see them. Then, as Truitt turned and rode toward the wagons, Jimmy finally saw movement. It was a child moving his arm.

The women and children were laying in the sand in the shade under the lead wagons. None of them seemed to have been shot, but the heat of the first three hours of the day without water had done its worst on them.

All of them moved closer, leading their horses to what little shade the wagons gave them, then dismounted.

Jimmy found one woman who looked to be about his mother's age. She was barely able to talk and he gave her a small sip of water. Her chapped lips struggled with the drink, but after a moment, some life returned to her eyes.

"Give everyone else some water," Jimmy said to the others, "see who is alive, who isn't."

"Don't give them too much water at first," Long said. "In their conditions, it will make them sick."

The boys spread out to the women and children laying under the wagons, waking them, giving them water.

"Jake Benson?" Jimmy asked the woman. "Did he do this?"

She nodded. "He and his men turned on us in the middle of the night. They said we were slowing them down. They robbed us, shot the men, then took all the water, stock, and money. They left us here to die."

Jimmy felt sick to his stomach. Benson was the most cold-hearted creature that had ever pretended to be human. How could anyone do this simply for money?

Jimmy gave the woman another small sip, then stood and went to talk to Zach and C.J.

"We have to get these women and children to the Truckee," Jimmy said.

"I can't see how we can," C.J. said.

"But we can't leave them," Zach said, echoing exactly what Jimmy was thinking.

"I know that," C.J. said. "But taking them may mean that none of us make it. We're still a long ways from that river."

Jimmy nodded. The sun was pounding on them. It felt like he had gotten far, far too close to a fire and there was no place to get away to.

"How far?" Jimmy asked.

C.J. shrugged. "From my guess, we are still a good fifteen, maybe twenty miles away from the river, through thick sand."

"And Long is going to want us to walk to save the horses," Zach said.

Jimmy didn't like the sound of that. "Find out how many women and children there are. And have Long check how much water we all have. Then we'll all talk. We're all risking our lives with this, we all need to be a part of this decision."

The rules of the west were that each person took care of themselves, but Jimmy had no doubt that he couldn't let these woman and children just die here. He was going to help them somehow, save them from what Benson had done.

He just hoped it didn't cost them all their lives.

★ PART TWENTY-EIGHT ★
TOUGH DECISION

"CAN WE JUST REST HERE in the shade of the wagons until the sun goes down and make a run for it?" Truitt asked as all six of them gathered together.

Jimmy had been wondering the same thing.

Long, C.J. and Josh all shook their heads.

"The heat on this desert would drain all of our water, even if we were resting," Josh said.

"Look what three hours did to the women and children," C.J. said. "And that was what one of them told me was their plan."

"We would never make it to the river without water," Josh said, "even at night."

Long agreed. In his steady voice he said simply, "We can't stop. We must press on and soon."

"How many are there?" Zach asked.

"Eight women still alive and all claim they are able to walk," Truitt said. "A dozen children, six of them too young to walk in this deep sand."

Jimmy turned to Long. "How much water do we have?"

"After what we have given to the women and children, we will be out of water before we get to the river, even if we went without them."

That made all of them stand in silence in the hot desert sun, just thinking about the huge risk they would take if they continued to help this wagon company.

Jimmy nodded, then looked around at his friends. "Is everyone agreed that we try to save these woman and children? I vote that we do."

All five of his friends nodded as one.

Jimmy laughed. "You know, we're all crazy."

"That seems clear simply by where we are standing," Truitt said.

Everyone laughed, but it was worried laughs. Jimmy was scared at the idea of what they were about to do. He knew the rest of them were as well.

"Everyone take a small drink," Jimmy said, "then give a small drink to the horses as well. After that, get the six kids who can't walk tied onto the horses so if they pass out, they won't fall off. We need to get moving."

Jimmy glanced in the direction of the hot sun as everyone spread out. It couldn't be much past nine in the morning. They had the hottest part of the day still hours ahead of them, and fifteen to twenty miles of sand to wade through.

And nowhere near enough water to get six of them, eight women, seven horses, and a dozen children to the Truckee River.

But they were going to try.

And with luck not die in the attempt.

⋆ PART TWENTY-NINE ⋆
AN ATTEMPT

THE NEXT TWO HOURS WENT slowly as the sun climbed higher and higher in the sky, sucking every bit of moisture from anything alive.

Long led the group, leading the only packhorse. The strongest woman among the survivors was leading Long's horse right behind him. A young boy was tied to the saddle, his head and back covered by a light shirt.

Jimmy, with a young girl on his horse, followed. A girl about Jimmy's age named Caroline walked with him, or behind him, as they tried to stay in the wagon wheel tracks to make the walking easier. It was Caroline's younger sister who was on Jimmy' horse.

Caroline was a blonde with flashing blue eyes. Her light skin was blistered by the sun, even though she wore a wide-brimmed hat. Her once blue dress was tattered, faded, and dirty. Jimmy liked her at once, but he wasn't sure why.

She seemed strong and was able to keep up. They didn't speak hardly at all, since that would have taken too much energy. But Jimmy found himself enjoying her company as much as it was possible in these circumstances. And thinking about her and wondering what she was like certainly kept his mind off of the heat and the deep sand.

After two hours, Long gave a little water to each horse, then had each of them take a very shallow drink. Jimmy had put him in charge of the water and told everyone to not drink unless Long told them to.

Jimmy was trusting Long to know when they had to drink to keep them going. Josh was also making a few suggestions to Long from things that he had read, and Long was sometimes following his suggestions.

Again, it was taking all of them and all their skills to survive this.

They didn't stop for longer than a few minutes at any point. There was just no point in resting. Every minute stopped was one minute longer it would take them to reach the river.

Before the next quick stop, Zach shouted from the end of the procession and Jimmy looked around.

A woman had fallen face first into the sand and two other women were not able to move her. It was the woman that Jimmy had given a drink to under the wagon.

Jimmy had Caroline hold his horse and he went back to see what could be done. But by the time he waded through the sand to where she was, C.J. was standing up shaking his head. "She's dead."

Two other women were still kneeling in the sand beside the dead woman.

Jimmy looked at the dead woman for a moment, the thoughts of his own mother filling his mind. Benson would pay for this. For everything he had done.

Jimmy turned his back on the dead woman. "Let's get moving."

He knew his voice sounded cold and mean, but he didn't dare allow himself to look back at her body just laying there beside the trail with all the other bones of travelers and horses and oxen.

They weren't crossing just a desert. They were crossing a graveyard.

An hour later, they were slugging up a low ridge. The sand was so deep, that even staying in the wagon wheel tracks from companies that had gone before, the horses sank up to their knees in the sand.

Every step for Jimmy seemed like torture.

Long stopped them halfway up the impossible slope and had them all drink tiny sips of the water they had left. Now they were completely out of water, and the sun was still high in the sky, baking them.

Jimmy just hoped there wasn't far to go. He could tell his energy was draining quickly, and beside him, Caroline was stumbling far more often than she had when they started out. He wasn't sure how many more miles any of them could go.

Over an hour later, they crested over the top of hill. The wagon trail went downward with a much harder base sand between some thin sagebrush. The going was easier, a relief since they were going downhill and not wading in such deep sand.

In the distance, in the bottom of the valley below them, there was a tall stand of cottonwood trees that seemed to curve off into the distance toward the mountains beyond. Jimmy had learned that distances out west were very hard to judge. He had no idea if those trees were just a mile away, or ten miles away.

But what those tall trees meant was water. The river was there, under those trees.

They just had to get to them.

★ PART THIRTY ★
THE RIVER

AS C.J. CAME OVER THE ridge behind Jimmy and saw the trees, he shouted, "Three miles left! Just three miles!"

Caroline looked back at C.J., then ahead at the trees. "Can he be right?"

Jimmy smiled. "When it comes to this trail and where we are, C.J. and Josh are always right. They've read everything about this trip that has ever been written. I have a hunch that Josh will eventually write his own book about all this as well."

"Three miles," Caroline said, her voice cracking in what sounded like a sigh. "I can make three miles."

She was right. Jimmy knew he could as well.

They walked on side-by-side in silence through the baking heat.

Long kept their pace steady and didn't speed up at all, even though it was downhill and they could see in the distance their goal. Jimmy knew that they could still lose people and horses in these three miles.

Three miles was a very long distance in this kind of heat.

But Long also didn't call a rest break half way down the gentle slope. At this point, there was no point in resting. They had no water left. They either made the last few miles, or they died very close to their goal.

Another woman behind Jimmy fell, but this time she hadn't died. Just passed out.

"I know what that's like," Truitt said, shaking his head.

Long and Zach simply lifted the woman up and draped her over Zach's horse in front of a small child. If she ended up dying, they would find out at the river and not before.

The last half-mile had to be the longest half-mile Jimmy had ever walked.

The cottonwood trees bordering the river were looming high in front of them now, and the blue of water reflected the sun like a mirror. But they were still a half-mile away under baking sun.

Every footstep felt like sheer agony, and Jimmy seemed to use every ounce of his energy with every step, yet the sight ahead kept him moving, taking another step forward and then another step.

Caroline was walking beside the horse and her sister, and it was clear that at times she was using his saddle to hold herself up from falling.

A few times during that last half mile, Jimmy turned to see how the others were doing.

They were all stumbling like he was, but they were all looking ahead at the water.

Long kept them going at the same speed all the way to within three hundred paces from the river, then he turned and shouted back, "Get the children off the horses without trying to stop the horses, then give the horses their heads."

Jimmy had no idea what Long was worried about with the children. All he wanted to do was stagger at the water and drink. But he didn't have enough energy to ask Long why. He just acted.

They all did.

Somehow, he and Caroline got her sister untied and off the horse without stopping. The little girl was completely limp in Jimmy' arms. Then Caroline tossed the reins back up over the horse's head so that it could go as it wanted.

Just as Jimmy had thought about doing, his horse made a dash at the river, splashing into it right behind Long's horse.

Caroline and Jimmy almost got run over by Truitt's horse as it went past, also headed for the water.

"Everyone drink slowly at first, just small sips." Long shouted, then turned for the river himself.

Jimmy somehow carried Caroline's small sister the last few hundred paces to the water's edge, then laid her gently on the wet rocks beside the water.

As Caroline was giving her sister a handful of water, washing the young girl's face, and taking a handful herself, Jimmy walked into the water and fell face first into the wonderfully cold, clear river.

Never, in all his life, had anything felt so wonderful.

Beside him, one after another, everyone did the same.

★ PART THIRTY-ONE ★
BACK INTO THE DESERT

JIMMY CRESTED OVER THE RIDGE and looked at the deadly Forty Mile Desert. Its rolling sand seemed to stretch forever.

He and his friends had just made it across that desert. They had barely escaped the intense heat and lack of water the first time across.

Now they were riding back into the desert.

Again.

Into the very good chance of death.

Again.

Jimmy felt more scared this time than the first time. Now he knew the dangers, and how close, very close, the desert had come to killing them all.

He remembered the intense agony of every step, the thirst, the feeling of fighting off losing consciousness and just falling into the hot sand.

Yet, within five days of beating the desert the first time, they were going to challenge it yet again.

This kind of stupidity he was sure was what got people killed in the west. And up until now, all of them working together had been pretty smart. At least, they had survived.

Challenging the Forty Mile Desert a second time wasn't smart.

After making it across the desert the first time, they had stayed for three days on the banks of the Truckee River, camping with the women and children they had rescued.

Jimmy had not minded camping next to the river that long since the time allowed him to get to know Caroline a little better. She was his age and her father had been killed in a river crossing in the Wyoming Territory. It was just Caroline, her mother, and her little sister trying to make it to a homestead they had in California. She had no idea what they were going to do next, now that their wagon and all their supplies were lost.

For the first two evenings, Jimmy and the rest of his friends had talked among themselves about giving up on their chase of the killer, Benson, and helping the women over the mountains and into California.

But by the third day, they still hadn't decided what to do.

Jimmy's goal was to track Benson and stop him, get the deed to the gold mine back, and make Benson pay somehow for killing his parents and all the other people he and his men had killed along the trail from Independence.

But at the same time, Jimmy couldn't leave these women and children alone without food or supplies.

Joshua had suggested they just stay near the river helping the women recover for a few days and an answer might present itself, but then, when pushed, he had just smiled and not said any more. He clearly had a plan, but he wasn't sharing that plan with any of the rest of them, no matter how much they pushed him.

His only comment was simply to say, "It's too crazy to talk about yet."

None of them had seemed to mind the stay at the river either. The shade of the big cottonwood trees and the coolness of the river kept them all comfortable.

Truitt spent his time learning how to cook new recipes from the women, which was just fine by Jimmy and the rest.

Zach struck up a friendship with a girl named Sandra, and they spent a couple evenings walking along the river bank after dinner.

Longfeather was just happy that they were giving the horses time to rest. His passion was clearly those seven horses, and keeping them well.

Josh spent most of his time with his feet dangling in the cool water writing in his notebook, and every time he finished a story, C.J. got to be the first to read it.

It was also Josh and C.J. who had enough reading to know some basic medical help for the older women who were slow to recover. Long as well had a few wilderness cures, as he called them, and they all three learned from one of the older women on how to treat sunburned skin.

So it was three days well spent, as far as Jimmy was concerned, even though they might be getting farther and farther behind Benson.

On the evening of the third day, the wagon company that they had helped save from Benson back on Goose Creek arrived at the river, all of them splashing into the water just as they had done when they had arrived, even though it turned out they hadn't run out of water.

They were all happy to see each other again, and over dinner that night, Jimmy told the new arrivals what Benson had done to the women's wagon company.

They were all shocked, and said they had wondered what happened when they saw the men and wagons.

It was at that point that Josh told everyone about his plan. With enough men and horses, Josh thought they could go back and rescue the women's wagons.

Jimmy hated the idea.

Hated it.

Period.

The last thing he wanted was to go back into that desert.

Ever.

If he had to go back east to get his brother, Luke, he would go north and go on the Oregon Trail before crossing that desert again. As far as he was concerned, Josh had lost his mind.

But the men from the second wagon company who had just come off the desert thought it was possible, and the light in Caroline's eyes at the thought of having her family things back made Jimmy keep his mouth shut and think about it.

After talking with Long about the horses, and thinking about it for a few hours, he knew Josh was right.

He still hated the idea.

But he knew it was a good idea to go back into the desert for this reason.

Two days later, after the new wagon company's horses were well rested and watered, they set Josh's plan in motion.

Zach, Long, and Jimmy took all seven of their horses and loaded them with water bags and canteens and enough food and salty jerky to last for a day.

Three men from the new wagon company also went with them with nine of their horses. The plan that Josh had come up with would save five of the women's wagons.

If it worked.

They left after dinner, as the air was starting to cool near the river.

As Jimmy rode out of camp with a wave from Caroline, his only hope was to see her and the river again.

★ PART THIRTY-TWO ★
THE PLAN

THE RIDE BACK TO THE women's wagons, on rested horses, actually didn't take very long. Going through the first time, it had seemed to take forever to walk from the wagons to the river. But being fresh, rested, and on horseback, riding fast and after dark, the ride back out into the desert took less than four hours.

That eased Jimmy' worries a little, but not much.

They were back in the middle of the sand and there were still a bunch of things that could go wrong.

Very wrong.

When they reached the women's wagons, the sun was not even starting to color the morning sky, but the moon gave them more than enough light to work by.

They emptied the personal possessions of the women from two of the most damaged wagons into the five wagons that seemed to be in the best shape. They shifted some of the load around so that two of the wagons were much lighter than the other three. Two wagons had to be pulled through the sand with just two horses each. The heavier wagons would have four horses in harness.

They moved the men that Benson had killed, and the two dead women, and laid them out to one side of the two wagons they were leaving behind.

Then, with a few words from one of the older men, Jimmy and C.J. and Zach covered the bodies with a little sand and put a makeshift cross near them. It was the best they could do for the dead in the little time they had dared spend.

Jimmy knew it was much more than most people who died on this desert got.

They didn't bother even covering the body of the dead killer. He wasn't worth their time as far as Jimmy was concerned. Jimmy was just glad that Benson only had one man left in his gang.

With everyone riding in the wagons, they headed back to the river before sunrise.

So far, the plan seemed to be going perfectly.

So far.

But the Forty Mile Desert was the most deadly stretch of trail that Jimmy could ever imagine. He wasn't about to go underestimating it now. Just being out on it again was crazy.

Zach drove one of the two light wagons with Jimmy riding along, since they were the two most inexperienced with wagons. Between the two of them, they managed to stay close to the wagon in front of them.

Long drove the other two-horse light wagon.

The men from the wagon company, with the experience of getting wagons all the way from Independence, drove the other three.

It got hot, very hot, sitting up on that wagon seat as the morning wore on and the sun climbed overhead.

Jimmy managed to keep his face in the shade of his hat and his hands and arms out of the sun as much as possible.

The sand kicked up by the horses pelted his skin like fine shot from a gun, and his eyes felt like they were coated in sandpaper.

Both he and Zach were constantly washing their eyes out.

The lead wagon driver drove the horses at a good pace and stopped every hour to rest them. Every hour they also rotated the horses between teams of two on the light wagons, and teams of four on the heavy wagons.

They all drank their fill of water, and gave the horses as much as they wanted as well. They had brought enough water with them to drink at that pace for a day. But if something happened to slow them down, they were going to have to cut back quickly.

Much to Jimmy's relief, nothing happened.

They crested over the rise above the river in just under ten hours, and were welcomed back into camp near the river with a wonderful dinner, just twenty-four hours from the time they had left.

The smile on Caroline's face that evening when she saw her family's things was worth the trip back into the desert for Jimmy. She had even kissed him on the cheek to thank him, and then she made sure that he promised to come by their new homestead outside of Sacramento.

It was a kiss that Jimmy would always remember, and a promise he planned on keeping.

★ PART THIRTY-THREE ★
BACK ON THE CHASE

THE NEXT DAY, JIMMY WAVED at Caroline one last time, and then he and his friends left the Truckee River and headed up into the hills for Virginia City. They still had to somehow find Benson again, and stop him from killing any more people.

And they had to get the gold mine deed from him.

The closer they had gotten to California and the gold fields of Northern Nevada and the Sierra Mountains, the more they had talked about finding gold and striking it rich. It was great campfire talk almost every night now.

As they crossed over the ridge outside of Virginia City, Jimmy wasn't sure what he had been expecting, but it sure wasn't the large booming town that faced them.

Virginia City seemed almost as large as Independence, and covered a wide hillside as well as stretching down into two valleys. There were mine tailings in giant piles in dozens of locations among the buildings, and there wasn't a tree to be seen anywhere near the town.

Dust from horses and wagons drifted over the town like smoke.

The place looked very hot, and very alive. Even from a mile out, they could hear the piano music from the saloons, and occasional gunshots echoed off the mountains behind the town.

"We need to find a place to camp," Jimmy said as they all sat on the ridge staring at the town.

"Most of the mining claims are down the valley to the south," Josh said.

"And right in the middle and under the city itself," C.J. said. "If we go west, beyond the town, and over those low ridges, we should find fresher water and a place to camp."

They talked for a minute about how they should go into town.

Long felt that it might be asking for trouble if he went right into town without first seeing how the residents of Virginia City treated Indians.

Jimmy didn't like that, but after Long insisted, he went along.

Long and Truitt turned west, leading the packhorse. The two of them would go around the large city, while Jimmy, Zach, C.J, and Josh rode into town. They would all meet near dusk a few miles outside of town on the Carson City wagon road that connected the two towns.

Twenty minutes later, the four of them rode into the center of Virginia City, Nevada, the most dangerous town that existed west of the Mississippi, looking for a deadly killer.

★ PART THIRTY-FOUR ★
THE SEARCH GOES ON

JIMMY HAD BEEN STUNNED AT the excitement, the energy, and the feel of Virginia City when they rode in that first day. It was very much like Independence, only with far more drunks and fighting. The mines and mine tailings seemed to be everywhere, bright brown scars on the rough land. The mineshafts riddled the ground right under Main Street.

Over half of the buildings along the main streets were two-story wood structures, and more were going up all around. Clearly, since there were no trees nearby, they were hauling in the lumber from some distance.

Long had been right to stay out of town. Jimmy soon discovered that a few years earlier, there had been a massive misunderstanding that had led to the building of Fort Churchill by the Army and then the Pyramid Lakes Indian battle. Feelings around town were still running hot on what had happened, so it was better that Long had just stayed on the sidelines.

There was no sign at all of Benson or his one remaining man.

They met back up with Long and Truitt, then made camp on a river a few miles upstream from Fort Churchill. The location gave them fresh water and was up against a rock wall that could be defended if for some reason they were attacked. Jimmy had a hunch that they would be using the camp for some time to come. It was going to take time to search for Benson.

Then, early the next day, with Long and Josh staying in the camp, the rest again went in search of Benson.

C.J. had suggested that they would cover more ground if they split up, so Jimmy and Truitt went into Virginia City. Zach and C.J. headed in the other direction for Carson City.

Unlike the search in Independence, this time more than Jimmy knew Benson on sight. They also knew who Benson's riding companion was, and what the men's two horses and saddles looked like.

That first day of the search was long and hot, and left Jimmy feeling frustrated. Suppose Benson had gone ahead and stayed on the trail and went on over the mountains to Sacramento. Now, after all the time on the river, he might already have the gold deed registered in his name. That night, Jimmy talked to the rest about his worry and suggested that maybe they should split up, with some of them riding for Sacramento.

None of them had agreed with Jimmy's fears. They were all convinced that Benson was still in the area. As C.J. had said, "It's certain he's here somewhere."

Josh said, "It wouldn't be in his character to move on. He's going to drink and spend the money he stole from the women's company before he leaves here, just as he has done every time before."

Jimmy still wasn't sure, but he felt better that at least they all agreed that staying and searching was the right thing to do.

So the next day, Jimmy and Zach and C.J. and Truitt stayed together instead of going two different directions. C.J. figured it was better that they cover one town per day completely and Jimmy had agreed. They planned to split up in each town.

As it turned out, it didn't take long to prove C.J. and Josh correct. Benson had stayed.

It was in Virginia City, as they rode into town just after dawn, that Jimmy spotted Jake Benson, the man Jimmy hated more than any man alive. Benson's horse was roped in front of a saloon and the murderer was just walking down the sidewalk as if he had no care in the world.

"That's Benson," Jimmy said to his friends, pointing at Benson's back.

"So that's what the poisoned snake looks like," Truitt said.

"Deadly and mean," Zach said.

Zach and Truitt had never seen Benson before, since they had been taking the only survivor of Benson's Goose Creek killings back to Fort Hall when Jimmy and the others saved the wagon train.

"That's him," Jimmy said, not even trying to hide the disgust in his voice.

They quickly dismounted and tied up their horses in front of a general store.

"Now what?" Zach asked.

"We follow him," Jimmy said. "From now on, he never leaves our sight. Any time of the day or night. We just have to wait for the right moment."

The others nodded and they all moved after Benson down the main street.

Jimmy could barely contain his anger. Right in front of him was the man who had killed his mother and father. And many others along the trail from Independence.

Jimmy had to stop Benson, but he had no idea how.

And it was clear that the others wanted to stop Benson almost as much as Jimmy did, after burying that family on Goose Creek, and those men and women in the desert.

Benson had left a trail of bodies in his wake and it seemed that Jimmy and his friends had been doing nothing but cleaning up after him and digging graves. If Jimmy had anything to say about it, that was going to stop right here in Virginia City.

Benson just kept walking, his boots rumbling on the wooden sidewalk like it didn't matter. He was almost swaggering.

It was clear to Jimmy that Benson believed no one was after him for all that he had done. That was good. Even after being chased off from that wagon train back on Goose Creek, Benson didn't feel threatened, which meant they still had surprise on their side.

"Split up," Jimmy said. "Truitt, you and Zach pace him down the other side of the street."

Truitt and Zach crossed over between two wagons while Jimmy and C.J. stayed behind Benson.

Jimmy had no idea what they would do now that they had found him, but one thing was for certain, they weren't going to lose sight of him again. They would be on him like a tick on a yard dog until Benson did something that would allow them to act.

Benson walked most of the length of the booming mining town, going by saloon door after saloon door. The wooden sidewalk ended and he kept on going downhill, out of the main part of town, passing some smaller buildings and a few large tents that housed different businesses.

Then finally, near the lower south edge of town, Benson turned into a small wooden-planked building that had a painted barber pole hanging on the front wall. The building was no bigger than a shack

145

and had been built up against a rock bluff. It had a tin roof. Jimmy couldn't imagine how hot that must make it inside the little shack in the middle of the day. Even with the front door standing open, Jimmy doubted Benson would be in there long.

"Stay here," Jimmy told C.J. "I'll be back.

Then, as if on a mission, he walked past the front of the shack and got a quick look inside, keeping his hat low on his head.

He then circled around, went back up the other side of the street, and met the others off to one side of the street in the shade, where Benson couldn't see them.

"It's only Benson in there with a barber," Jimmy said. "Any ideas?"

Zach shook his head, as did Truitt.

But C.J. smiled. "I just might have something we could do. But if it fails, we might get shot."

"After watching that scum of the earth walk up the street like he had done nothing," Jimmy said, "I'm willing to take some risks. That man in that building killed my parents."

Zach nodded. "And a lot of other innocent people. After seeing how he left those women out in the desert to die, I agree. We have to stop this animal."

"All right," C.J. said, nodding. "But my plan is going to take some rope and a blanket."

Jimmy glanced around. There was a general store about a half block back up the street. He had maybe just enough money left for what C.J. needed. "You three stay here," he said. "How much rope?"

"Thin and strong and about thirty feet."

Jimmy nodded and turned toward the store without even asking C.J. what his plan was.

"Get a shovel, too," C.J. called after him. "With a long handle."

★ PART THIRTY-FIVE ★
THE PLAN

JIMMY TRUSTED C.J., BUT HE sure hoped this plan would work as he headed for the general store at a fast walk. They had rope on their horses, and blankets and shovels back in their camp, but that would take far too long to get. He was going to have to spend the very last of his father's money for this. He sure hoped it worked.

It took him less than five minutes and he was back with what C.J. said he needed.

C.J. took the shovel, gave the blanket to Truitt. Then he quickly explained his idea on how they could capture Benson and maybe get him to the Virginia City Sheriff. After they captured Benson, the boys would have to ride to catch the women in the wagon train. The women could then testify to the Sheriff about what Benson had done to their men. Jimmy was sure the women hadn't made it too far up into the Sierras yet.

"This is crazy," Zach said, smiling at Jimmy. "He has a gun and clearly doesn't mind killing people."

"I know," Jimmy said. "But we got to try."

"I'm not saying we don't," Zach said. "I'm just saying that this is crazy."

"No argument from me," Jimmy said, smiling back at his friend.

"You know," Truitt said as they headed across the street, "that if this works, we're going to have to come up with a name for it."

"Let's see if it works, first," C.J. said, clearly worried, even though it was his idea.

Near the barbershop, with the rope trailing behind him in the dirt, Jimmy walked past, again keeping his face from being seen clearly.

Inside the barbershop, he could see Benson still sitting in the chair and the barber working at Benson's beard and hair. Both were looking away from the door.

As Jimmy got to the other side of the barbershop and out of sight of Benson and the barber, he stopped and eased the rope right up near the front step up into the small shack.

On the other end of the rope, Zach pulled tight. To Jimmy, the rope seemed clearly obvious tucked against the bottom of the step, but C.J. had assured them that if they got Benson to come out fast and hard, he wouldn't notice it.

Truitt unfolded the dark wool blanket that Jimmy had bought and moved over against the barbershop front wall, his back to the wooden planks, the blanket held in both hands.

Then, when he was ready, it was C.J.'s turn.

C.J. stepped up so he could be seen through the front door of the small shack.

"You Jake Benson, mister?" C.J. asked, leaning on the shovel like he always stood that way.

Jimmy was impressed that C.J. sounded so calm, like none of this mattered.

"Yeah, what's it to ya, kid?" Benson said from inside.

Jimmy felt a chill go up his spine. He hadn't heard that voice since before his parents were killed. He hadn't liked it then, he didn't like it now.

"I was told to come down here and tell you that he's taking your horse and gear in payment for what you owe him."

"Who!" Benson shouted.

The shout echoed off the tin roof.

Jimmy could hear from the scraping sounds that Benson had stood up. Both Jimmy and Zach made sure they were braced and ready with the rope.

"He didn't give me his name," C.J. said. "Black beard, brown hat, black mare with a silver braid on the saddle."

C.J. had just described Benson's remaining riding companion.

With that, C.J. stepped back a few steps into the middle of the street, allowing room for Benson to come straight out of the building.

"I'll kill that snake," Benson shouted as he stormed out of the barbershop, putting his hat on as he came.

Jimmy and Zach instantly yanked the rope up as Benson stepped for the street. The rope caught him in the shin and Benson went forward hard, face down into the dust.

Truitt moved faster than Jimmy thought possible, sprawling on Benson from behind with the blanket, covering the killer's head and arms.

Zach and Jimmy moved in and quickly wrapped more of the rope around Benson's legs.

But Benson was clearly fast and angry. He was bucking Truitt like a wild horse out of control.

From under the blanket, Benson's hand and gun came out and he fired once.

The shot barely missed Jimmy and ricocheted off some rocks down the street.

"Get his gun!" Zach shouted.

Jimmy, as hard as he could, smashed his boot down on Benson's gun hand.

The gun spun away in the dirt.

Benson screamed and bucked Truitt even harder under the blanket, but couldn't stand because Zach has his legs tied up.

C.J. stepped up, and with a swing of the shovel, hit Benson on the head through the blanket.

Now Jimmy understood why C.J. had wanted the shovel.

Suddenly, Truitt was lying on an unmoving pile of man and blanket.

Jimmy's heart was beating so fast, he could hardly breathe, and he was sweating like he had never sweated before.

Truitt pulled the blanket off and stood while Zach wrapped even more rope around Benson's legs and tied it off like he would a steer.

They had captured Benson.

Jimmy couldn't believe it.

★ PART THIRTY-SIX ★
NOW WHAT?

"Everyone all right?" Jimmy asked.

"Yeah," they all said, but it was clear that Truitt was out of breath and likely bruised up from his ride on Benson's back.

Jimmy moved over and picked up the gun, holding the heavy hunk of metal in his hands. More than likely, this was the gun that had killed his parents, shot his mother in the back, killed the family at Goose Creek, and the men in the desert.

Jimmy looked at the gun, then at the man out cold in the dirt of the street.

"Shoot him," C.J. said. "Don't let him ever kill anyone again."

"We wouldn't blame you," Truitt said, "after what he did to your parents."

"This man do something to you boys?" the barber asked from the door of his shop.

"Killed my parents," Jimmy said, his voice surprisingly calm for how his stomach was feeling. "Shot my mother in the back."

"Oh," the barber said.

"And then he killed a family back on Goose Creek," Zach said. "And some men in the middle of the desert, leaving women and children to die just so he could steal their money and stock."

The barber nodded. "You know, a lot goes on in this street that I just don't seem to notice."

Then the man turned and went back into his shack, cleaning, pretending to not look out the door.

Truitt laughed.

Jimmy was just glad that the barber wasn't going to try to stop them. Jimmy stared at Benson, then at the gun in his hands. He really wanted to kill Benson. More than he had wanted to kill anything or anyone in his entire life.

But he wouldn't do it.

He was still bothered by the man they had accidentally killed back on Goose Creek. Killing Benson would give him nightmares for the rest of his life.

And besides that, it wasn't the right thing to do.

He shook his head, still staring at the heavy gun in his hands.

"No, I'd be just like him if I killed him," Jimmy said. "For whatever the reason."

Jimmy unloaded the revolver and then laid it on a rock beside the barbershop. Picking up another large rock, he smashed the gun over and over, feeling the anger toward Benson with every blow.

The gun was shattered and bent and in pieces when he finally stopped.

"No one is going to be killed by that gun again," Jimmy said, panting at the work it had taken to destroy the gun.

"There isn't a big enough piece left to throw at anyone," Truitt said, laughing.

Jimmy turned back to see the rest of them all smiling at him. Along the street, a small crowd was gathering to watch.

To Jimmy, it didn't matter. Benson would never kill another person with that gun.

★ PART THIRTY-SEVEN ★
TRYING TO GET THE MINE BACK

BENSON MOANED AND TRIED TO push himself to his feet, realizing slowly that his hand was injured and his feet tied.

Jimmy moved over to Benson, who looked up at him from his hands and knees.

"Remember me?" Jimmy asked.

Benson blinked a few times, then suddenly he remembered. "The Tyler kid."

Jimmy nodded. "Good, I was hoping you would remember, since you killed my mother and father."

Benson snorted and said, "We're a long way from Missouri, kid." He turned around so that he could work to untie the ropes around his feet.

"Before my mother died from the two bullets you put in her back," Jimmy said, "she told me and my brother it was you. Now I would like my father's gold mine deed back that you stole."

Benson snorted again. "Tough woman, your mother."

Benson kicked the rope loose and tried to push himself to his feet, wincing at the pain in his hand as he braced himself with it.

With all the anger that had built up over the past few months, Jimmy stepped forward and stamped down hard on Benson's gun hand again, smashing it into the ground.

The tough man screamed and fell back into the dirt, clenching his broken hand.

"I'm going to kill you, kid," Benson said through clenched teeth, his eyes closed in pain as he rolled in the dirt.

"Not with that hand you're not," Jimmy said. "So, my father's gold mine deed, please."

"You going to have to kill me before you get that gold mine deed back, kid," Benson said.

"Oh, we're going to do much worse than that," Jimmy said.

Jimmy glanced at C.J. who was standing in the street behind Benson. "Want to help our guest rest for a few more minutes?"

"I would love to," C.J. said, smiling.

When Benson moved to sit back up, C.J. stepped forward and hit Benson from behind on the side of the head with the flat base of the shovel. The clang echoed down the street and the few of the town's people who were watching and listening made laughing noises as Benson flopped out cold in the dirt.

"Remind me next time we're digging," Truitt said to C.J., "that you're deadly with a shovel."

"Thank you," C.J. said, smiling and pretending to bow like he was performing in a Wild West show.

"Truitt, keep an eye out for this guy's riding companion," Jimmy said.

"Yeah, real good thinking," Truitt said, moving up the street closer to town. He jumped up on a rock so that he could see over the growing crowd.

155

By now, people were watching from both sides of the street and close enough to hear everything that was said. Jimmy didn't care. At this point, he had nothing to hide.

Zach wrapped the rope around Benson's feet again, and tied it off solid. It would take a knife to get that rope off the next time.

"Remind me to not get you men mad at me," the barber said from his doorway.

Benson's damaged hand was flopped in the dirt. It was clearly broken at the wrist and already starting to swell.

Jimmy, with his mother and father's dead bodies in his mind, stepped forward and smashed Benson's gun hand again with the heel of his boot.

Bone snapped loud enough to echo down the street.

Around them, the crowd made a gasping noise.

"Oh, that's got to hurt," C.J. said.

Jimmy smashed Benson's hand once more, grinding it under the heal of his boot just to make sure the man would never use that hand for anything, let alone firing a gun to kill anyone.

To Jimmy, what he was doing didn't feel good. But it felt right.

★ PART THIRTY-EIGHT ★
A SECOND ATTEMPT

THE PAIN OF THE SECOND stamping woke Benson up and he screamed again, clutching his forever-useless hand to his chest and rolling in pain in the street.

Finally, after what seemed like a long time of cursing and shouting, Benson sat up and tried to untie the ropes with his one good hand.

Jimmy kneeled down to face the man who had killed his parents.

"Now, the deed to the gold mine that you stole from my father after you killed him and my mother. Where is it?"

Jimmy made sure his voice was loud enough for anyone in the crowd to hear.

"Never," Benson said through the pain.

"It's all right for you to kill anyone you want," Jimmy said, shaking his head and laughing. "But you can't take a little pain?"

Benson glared at Jimmy.

Jimmy decided to try another way to get the mine. "You know, all those women and children you left in the Forty Mile Desert without water are going to be really happy to see you."

Jimmy made sure his voice was loud. He wanted everyone to know what this man had done.

Benson again just glared at him.

Jimmy went on. "Especially since you gunned down their fathers and husbands and stole all their water and stock. What do you think they're going to tell the sheriff when they see you?"

A couple people in the crowd gasped.

"They're dead," Benson said, trying to spit at Jimmy and missing.

"No," Jimmy said, "actually, they are all alive. My friends and I were behind you, and we saved them. And they are all very willing to tell the sheriff what you did. Now, where is my father's gold mine deed?"

"Never," Benson said. "I said never, kid, and I mean never. You're going to die for what you have done to me."

"Oh, you're going to shoot me in the back like you did my mother?" Jimmy asked, not bothering to hide the anger in his very loud voice.

Benson tried to spit again, but nothing seemed to come out of his mouth.

"Listen," Jimmy said, "you think what we did to you here is bad, in front of all these fine people?"

Benson twisted around, suddenly realizing that a crowd had gathered to listen and watch and no one was helping him.

Jimmy went on. "You'll discover this is nothing. We're going to dog you every step you take, every moment of every day and night and make your life a living nightmare until we get my father's gold mine deed back."

"Just try it, kid. You'll make it easier for me to kill you."

"Just remember I warned you," Jimmy said.

Jimmy stood up as Benson struggled to untie the ropes around his ankles with one hand.

Jimmy nodded to C.J., who smiled and once again hit Benson on the back of the head with the flat of the shovel.

Benson went over sideways in the dirt.

The crowd cheered this time.

"He's going to have one very nasty headache," Zach said, laughing.

⋆ PART THIRTY-NINE ⋆
DOING THE RIGHT THING

JIMMY QUICKLY SEARCHED BENSON, NOT enjoying the feel of touching the man at all, but he had to look for the gold mine deed.

Nothing.

"Search him to see if I missed it," Jimmy said to Zach.

Zach found only a few coins that he pocketed. But no gold mine deed.

"So, we going to turn him into the sheriff?" C.J. asked.

"I think that's what he deserves, don't you?" Jimmy asked. "Then we have to go see if we can catch the women's wagons before they get too far up the Truckee. They will need to stand witness against him for what he did to their husbands and fathers."

"Good answer, kid," a voice said from the crowd as a man stepped forward.

Jimmy turned to see the sheriff of Virginia City walking toward him. He was a tall man, very thin, with rough skin on his face and a scar on his forehead. But the smile on the sheriff's face told Jimmy that he was in no trouble.

"Sir," Jimmy said, "are you willing to hold him until we get the women to come and testify against him?" Jimmy asked.

"We know he's killed at least ten men in Nevada," C.J. said.

Again the crowd gasped.

The sheriff stood over Benson and shook his head in disgust, then turned to Jimmy. "You boys bring witnesses to a crime this man committed and we'll put him on trial. Nevada Circuit Court rides through here in three days."

"Thank you, Sheriff," Jimmy said, smiling.

The sheriff glanced around and motioned for two men to come help him carry Benson. "Better stop at Doc's office to get him to take care of the hand," the sheriff said, smiling. "Looks to me like he caught it between two rocks."

The crowd just laughed.

Jimmy felt very, very relieved.

It was over.

Jimmy and Zach went back up the street until they found Benson's horse and searched his saddlebags. No mining deed. But they did find a few things that would help them, and a little more money tucked down in a hidden pocket.

"Now how do we find it?" Truitt asked as Benson was led off to jail.

"We find Benson's friend and follow him back to their camp," Jimmy said. "It must be in his gear at his camp."

They searched all afternoon through the city, and never spotted Benson's friend.

But to Jimmy, the mine didn't seem to matter that much at the moment. They had stopped a killer.

And Benson would be tried.

And Jimmy would get to see Caroline again.

It surprised him how much he wanted to see her, be around her.

That night, they celebrated around their campfire.

Jimmy knew that his brother Luke would be proud of what he had done, the lives they had saved by stopping Benson.

It felt very, very good.

Josh made C.J. tell him three times what had happened so that he could write it all down, and then made C.J. promise that the next day he would take Josh into Virginia City to see the area in front of the barbershop, so he could get it right in the story.

Jimmy just sat there and enjoyed his friends.

Enjoyed making it west.

He had set out to have an adventure and it had been far more than he had ever wanted. But they all had survived and helped others.

Since losing his parents, it was the best night Jimmy had had.

In the next Buffalo Jimmy adventure,
Jimmy and his friends continue on into California,
tracking Benson's killer friend. And finding trouble
far worse than they had ever expected.

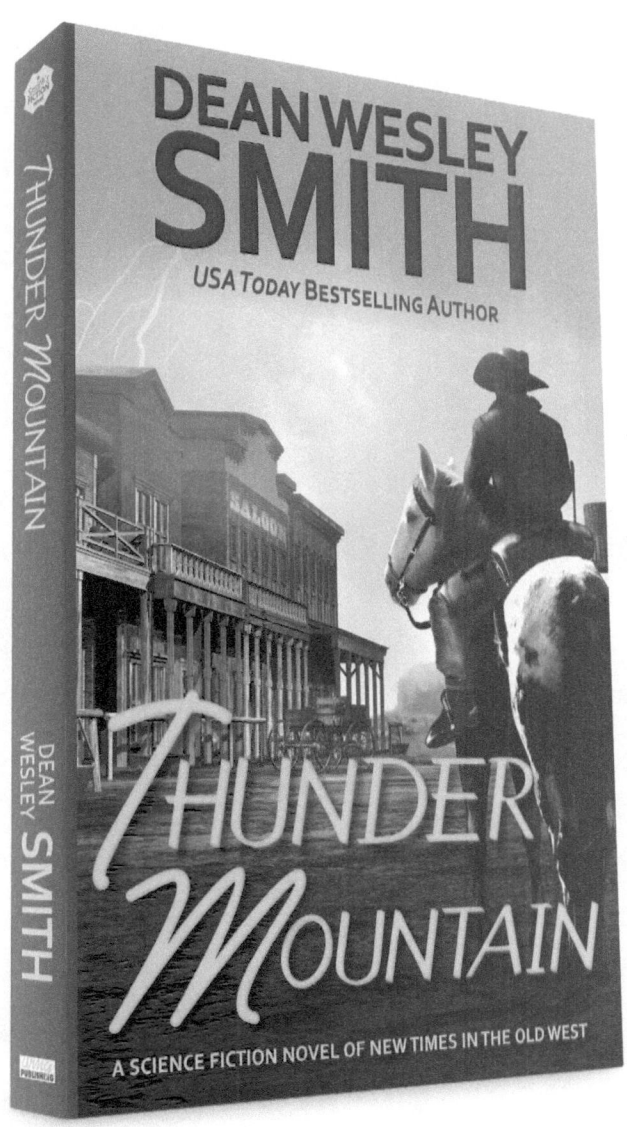

Want to read about more adventures in the Old West, try Dean Wesley Smith's Thunder Mountain series, beginning with *Thunder Mountain*, available now from your favorite bookseller.

ABOUT THE AUTHOR

USA Today bestselling author Dean Wesley Smith has published more than a hundred novels in thirty years and hundreds and hundreds of short stories across many genres.

He wrote a couple dozen *Star Trek* novels, the only two original *Men in Black* novels, Spider-Man and X-Men novels, plus novels set in gaming and television worlds. He wrote novels under dozens of pen names in the worlds of comic books and movies, including novelizations of a dozen films, from *The Final Fantasy* to *Steel* to *Rundown*.

He now writes his own original fiction under just the one name, Dean Wesley Smith. In addition to his upcoming novel releases, his monthly magazine called *Smith's Monthly* premiered October 1, 2013, filled entirely with his original novels and stories.

Dean also worked as an editor and publisher, first at Pulphouse Publishing, then for *VB Tech Journal*, then for Pocket Books. He now plays a role as an executive editor for the original anthology series *Fiction River*.

To learn more about his latest projects, go to www.deanwesley smith.com.

www.ingramcontent.com/pod-product-compliance
Lightning Source LLC
Chambersburg PA
CBHW022124170626
46808CB00002B/829